GHOST BUS

GHOST BUS

Tales from Wellington's Dark Side

by

Anna Kirtlan

First published in New Zealand in 2020

Text copyright © Anna Kirtlan, 2020
seamunchkin.com

This is a work of fiction. Names, characters, businesses, places, events and incidents are either the product of the author's overactive imagination or used in a fictitious manner. With the exception of public figures any resemblance to persons living or dead is coincidental and the drunk engineer who helps fix an alien spaceship is most definitely not based on my partner.

ISBN 978-0-473-52548-4
also available as an ebook

Cover design: Catherine Slavova – Karnstein Designs
Editing and Typesetting: Jana Mittelstädt – Kiwiberry Editing

TABLE OF CONTENTS

This book is dedicated to Mr Pies.
The best ghost a girl could have.

INTRODUCTION

This collection of stories started life as a National Novel Writing Month entry. While I didn't finish the 50,000 words needed to complete the challenge, I did end up with a sort of warped love letter to Wellington.

Some of these stories are spooky, some are silly, and some have a pretty high body count, but all of them will, I hope, in some way make you smile. They are escapism, pure and simple – my gift to a world that might just need a little bit of that right now.

This is my first foray into fiction, but when I was putting this together for publication, it wasn't the ghosts, aliens and witches that stood out – it was the normal things that aren't so normal anymore. Hanging out in book stores, catching a packed bus, buying a kebab at 3am.

What this book has actually turned out to be is a love letter to a Wellington that was – a Wellington I miss, and one I very much look forward to seeing again.

Thanks to my editor Jana Mittelstädt for helping me shape this bundle of strangeness and to Catherine Slavova for the stunning cover. A shout out, too, to the Wellington Sculpture Trust for making the research for the first story incredibly easy. I apologise for what I have done with your beloved sculptures.

Anna Kirtlan, May 2020.

The Ministry for Public Art

Dedicated to the Wellington Sculpture Trust

It's amazing how short people's memories can be or perhaps – to be more charitable – how quickly we protect ourselves by blocking out traumatic events.

I can understand it coming from tourists, but when locals ask why we have so many statues of women outside parliament, I must admit it makes me a little afraid.

It was October 7, 2018 when the Len Lye kinetic sculpture, the Water Whirler, was snapped in two on Wellington's waterfront. The sculpture wasn't even running at the time. It was fenced off and under maintenance when a tourist took it into his head to climb it. As it gave way, he plummeted into the water, whacking his head on the way down.

The culprit, a man in his 20s, got away with a gash on his forehead, a $1000 fine and a whole lot of public outrage. Through the power of social media, he was tracked down and interviewed. His reason for assaulting the artwork? He was bored.

The second time, the Water Whirler ended up in the news was much more gruesome. A couple were walking along the waterfront when they noticed something looked off in the area the sculpture was situated. On closer inspection they saw that, once again, it had been moved from the base. This time though, it had company.

The Water Whirler was doubled over but it hadn't snapped. Instead, something was holding it up. That something was a young man. The pointed end of the sculpture had pierced right through his chest, leaving him dangling there with bulging eyes and gaping mouth. The amount of blood pooling at the bottom of the artwork left no doubt there had been no chance of survival.

How am I able to describe the scene in such detail? Well, other than the couple who discovered him, I was one of the first on the scene.

I'm a photographer. One of the few specialists still employed by the news media. However, with the popularity of point and shoot digital cameras, the quality of lenses on phones and the multi-tasking journalists are expected to do these days, work has dried up a bit. So, to make ends meet, I double as an on-call snapper for the police when they need it.

I can tell you right now I have seen some things. But nothing will ever top that month – the October that began with the Water Whirler.

The crime scene investigation threw up nothing. No witnesses, no prints, no obvious enemies. I'm only the photographer but I still pick up on things, and what I picked up was that the constabulary were utterly bamboozled.

Of course, the rumour mill kicked into gear. It was someone hired by the sculptor's family or art fanatics getting revenge. Though none of those people were particularly well known for their capacity for brutal murder.

The second crime scene I was dispatched to that week was eerily similar. The first sign of disturbance was a statue out of place and next to it, someone who was definitely quite dead.

This time, it was the Fruits of the Garden statue situated above Frank Kitts Park. Sculpted in bronze by Paul Dibble, it includes ferns and a woman's torso, chopped above the belly button and below the thighs, with an apple balanced on top. To be honest, I had always found it a little creepy, though I would never say that out loud now.

If you didn't know what the statue was supposed to look like, you could be forgiven for not noticing anything was amiss. A more eagle-eyed public sculpture enthusiast, however, would pick up fairly quickly that the apple had gone AWOL. The dead body lying on the ground with a bronze apple shoved in the vicinity of its mouth would have been the giveaway for the rest of us.

I say 'in the vicinity' because, while the obvious intention was for the apple to be shoved in the victim's gob, the fruit in question was much too large for a human jaw and the end result had destroyed most of the unfortunate chap's face.

There are some things that are best not described in detail, and this is one of them. As I said before, I have seen some things, but that was the first crime scene I had shot where I had to quietly go and vomit in the bushes once I was done.

By now, the media was having a field day. Wellington had a serial killer with a statue fetish on its hands. Kooky conspiracy theories abounded on social media and parents banned their kids from going to town. Two days later though, and even the wildest speculations were blown out of the water.

***

I was walking along the waterfront, as I do most mornings, when I heard an ear-splitting scream followed by a splash.

"That is the last fucking time someone sticks a novelty hat on me!" a male voice roared.

I looked towards the source of the yelling to see the most bat crap crazy thing I had ever clapped my eyes on – up to that point. A cast iron, naked man had a tourist in a headlock while dangling another over the ocean by his wrist. A sparkly fluorescent green fedora and feather boa were floating in the harbour while two phones were in the process of sinking.

The phrase 'cast iron' is not a euphemism either. The man in question was actually made of metal. He was Wellington's iconic Solace in the Wind statue. A two-metre-tall iron representation of a naked man leaning into the wind over the harbour, his arms flung back as he embraces the elements.

Created by sculptor Max Pattè, he is arguably Wellington's most photographed statue. The sight of tourists posing next to him, leaning towards the water with him – and undoubtedly falling into the drink on occasion – was just part of the parcel of a Wellington waterfront walk.

He was also one of Wellington's most dressed up statues. Santa hats at Christmas, bunny ears at Easter, all manner of ridiculous get-ups when Wellington hosted the Rugby Sevens. It appeared the unfortunate duo the statue was yelling at had attempted to dress him up in dollar store party gear for a photo shoot.

"Take your selfies. That's fine, flattering even, but stop sticking crap on me. Show some damned respect!"

Trying to process what I was witnessing, I stepped forward, distracting him mid-rant. It was lucky for the tourist he was dangling over the ocean that I did because if the statue had tightened his grip any harder, he could have broken the man's wrist.

Dropping his victim disdainfully into the harbour, Solace turned to the other tourist in his grasp.

"NO MORE PARTY HATS!" he roared. "Tell your friends!"

Sniffing in disgust, the statue tossed his victim aside. In all his naked glory, Solace in the Wind strode off towards the city, leaving a quivering pile of human on the pavement and another flailing in the ocean.

"Can you swim?" I yelled to the man in the water, after checking that his friend, while hysterical, was going to survive.

"Yes!" he sputtered.

"Swim over to me. There's a ladder right here you can use to climb out," I yelled, leading him to the exit point, most likely put there for photography accidents by the council. I helped haul him up the ladder and reunited him with his friend. Both clearly in shock, I called an ambulance to make sure they'd be okay.

At this stage, quite a crowd of concerned onlookers had converged on the pair. I waited with the statue's victims until help arrived, trying to explain as best I could what had happened without sounding like an utter lunatic. The complete absence of a statue was at least one point in my favour.

Once satisfied the pair were in good hands, I walked in the direction Solace had headed, in a bid to find out what was going on.

*****

It wasn't hard to work out where to go next. All I needed to do was follow the screaming.

The bulk of the noise was coming from the City to Sea Bridge – a shortcut from the waterfront to Civic Square and through to the CBD. The first thing I noticed was that most of it was gone.

The bridge was constructed around a number of wooden sculptures created by artist Paratene Matchitt. One side of the bridge was formed by two whale-shaped taniwha called Ngake and Whātaitai and the other by two massive birds.

It was one of the latter I was watching circle the skies with two screaming people dangling from its beak. As I stared slack-jawed, the second bird appeared over the horizon, zeroing in on those of us left on the bridge.

I'm not proud of what I did next, but there was absolutely nothing I could have done to help the people around me. I put my head down, made myself as small as possible and ran.

I must have avoided the giant bird's gaze because I made it to Civic Square unscathed, right into the centre of another chaotic scene.

Neil Dawson's fern orb is a silver sphere that is usually suspended by wires above the square. On a good day, it appears to float among the clouds. That day however, it was far from the sky. Instead, it was rolling along the ground, knocking people aside like skittles.

At first, it seemed its movements were erratic, but the longer I watched the more targeted they appeared. When it reached the end of each destructive run, it would line itself up and aim for the densest points in the scattering crowd.

I watched in horror as handbags and shoes flew across the square. Again, I made myself as small as possible and thankfully escaped notice as the orb rolled past, out of the square and towards the city.

Why was I moving towards the danger? Honestly, I don't know. It's not as though I even had my camera on me. Any photos I took that day were with my phone. I suspect being a photographer is similar to being a journalist. We have an innate sense of nosiness, a need to understand what is going on and, I suspect, a touch of FOMO.

Either way, there I was heading towards the CBD, and a bunch of murderous statues.

***

Willis Street was pretty quiet. I guess because there isn't a huge amount of art there. As soon as I turned the corner to Lambton Quay however, I had the wind knocked out of me. Literally. One minute I was peering cautiously down the street, and the next I was doubled over on the ground gasping for air. I looked around to see who, or what, was attached to the fist that had just connected with my stomach and came eyeball to snout with a bronze beagle.

It took a dazed minute or two before I recognised the snarling little beast as Fritz, the canine companion of John Plimmer from the Plimmer and His Dog statue. I looked across the road and sure enough, there was the so-called 'father of Wellington', his top hat at a jaunty angle as he kneecapped passers-by with his walking stick. I jumped to my feet before Fritz could take the bite he so obviously wanted to and aimed a kick at the little dog's head, reasoning with myself that it wasn't animal abuse when the animal was made of bronze. Growling, he took off down the street in search of easier targets, stopping on occasion to pee on lamp posts.

I carefully crept down Lambton Quay, ducking into shop doorways as enraged sculptures of all types surged past. It felt like a protest march of some description. All that was missing were banners and megaphones.

A metallic cry followed by an unholy chorus of screaming interrupted my thoughts. Behind me was an H G Wells nightmare.

The tripod sculpture from the top of Courtney Place, which had always given me the heebie-jeebies, was stalking its way down the road. An obvious homage to the War of the Worlds Martian warships, the steampunk-style monstrosity created by Weta Workshop loomed over terrified pedestrians.

The metallic shriek started up again as its 'head', cleverly shaped like a video camera, jerked to one side. A camera bulb flash was followed by a stream of flame so hot no-one near it stood a chance. Like some sort of demented cyborg dragon, the tripod's literal heat ray fried everyone in its path. The only saving grace was that death was instantaneous. One minute, people were running and screaming and the next, they were a pile of ash on the footpath.

I didn't look where I was running. I just ran, ducking behind a solid structure just as the metal monster picked its way past, miraculously not spotting me. I looked up in time to see one of its legs towering over me. This close up, I could see that what looked like mechanical components were actually gaming consoles – Nintendo 64 controllers and Gameboys. Literal revenge of the nerds. And was that? A toasted sandwich maker? I held my breath as it stepped over me and continued down the street.

***

I ducked out from my hiding place behind, oh god, another statue. It was Katherine Mansfield this time – or to give her proper title, Woman of Words. Three metres of marine-grade stainless steel covered in cut-out passages of her writing (her hair is actually made of shopping lists found in her journals). Lit up from within at night, she is beautiful but also quietly terrifying.

I braced myself for an assault, but luckily, she seemed preoccupied.

"Got you!" she shouted triumphantly, clutching a seagull that had dared land on her head. "I will not have you little sods shitting on me anymore!"

I watched in horrified fascination as her mouth stretched open to reveal a row of razor-sharp teeth. The seagull gave one final hapless squawk before Katherine's mouth clamped down, severing head from body. She spat out the head in disgust and tossed the corpse to the ground.

I was too close to her to sneak past and, having witnessed the other statues' sudden speedy mobility, I was pretty sure I wouldn't be able to outrun her. So, that left one option: talk my way out of the situation.

"Katherine, ah, Miss Mansfield," I said, stepping out from behind her skirts.

"Katherine is fine," she replied, picking feathers from her teeth.

"Katherine, would you mind telling me what's going on?" I asked. "Why are the statues killing everyone?"

She looked down at me, daintily wiping the last of the seagull blood from her chin as her mouth stretched into a grin.

"We were bored."

Bored. My first reaction was sheer outrage.

"Yes, bored. Like that vile young man who snapped a waterfront work of art in two," she snapped haughtily.

A sick realisation crept over me.

"This is about that kid breaking the water wand?" I asked.

"Water Whirler," Katherine corrected. "And that particular incident was the last straw. We are done with being dressed up, graffitied ..." she shot the dead seagull a look of disgust, "shat on."

"We have had it with people smoking and fornicating behind us, and don't even get me started on the people who cover themselves in paint and pretend to be us!"

I stared in stunned silence. I had honestly never thought about how badly we treated our public art before.

"And then, there's the representation issue," she continued, warming to her subject.

"Representation issue?" I asked, partly because the longer she was talking the less likely she was to rip my head off, but also because I was genuinely interested.

"Yes! How many female statues have you seen around the city?"

I tried to think. She was right. It was definitely a bit of a boys' club.

"Two!" she answered for me. "There are two. And before I came along in 2015, there was just one."

"No way!" I replied, genuinely shocked.

"Yes way!"

"Who was the first one?"

Katherine turned and gestured back down the quay. "Her," she said, smiling broadly.

Sweeping imperiously down the street, swatting people indiscriminately with her sceptre, was none other than Queen Victoria.

I had only ever seen her glowering down from atop her towering plinth between Kent and Cambridge terraces. Up close, she was even more imposing.

Queen Vic was Wellington's first significant sculpture, created between 1902 and 1905 by Alfred Drury, following an outpouring of imperial sentiment after her death (and a determination to have a bigger statue of her than the one in Auckland.) She was moved from her original spot in Post Office Square after being declared a traffic hazard once the trams arrived, and that wasn't the only ignominy she suffered according to Katherine.

"They painted her brown in the 1920s and gold in the 40s," she whispered conspiratorially as Her Majesty approached. "She's still pissed about that."

I dropped to one knee as the queen bore down on us.

"Wise move," Katherine said approvingly.

"Your Majesty," Katherine said, curtseying as the queen paused in her rampage to acknowledge her.

"Sister," Victoria responded. "I swung past my old stomping ground," the queen continued, ignoring me. "Hate what they have done with the place."

I assumed she was talking about Post Office Square.

"I had to listen to those tedious little people making their protest speeches below me for so long while I was there. Now, it's my turn!" she finished with a glint in her eye.

"Our turn, sister", Katherine said with a diabolical grin.

"Indeed," Victoria agreed, gathering up her voluminous skirts and sweeping off down the street.

"Where's she going?" I asked, straightening myself up. "Where are they all going?" I added as I watched the parade of public art filing past.

"Parliament!" Katherine cried gleefully. "And if we don't hurry up, we'll miss out on all the fun!"

Before I could blink, she had swept me up in her metal arms and carted me off down the street like a child. It was by turns humiliating and exhilarating.

"Um, Katherine," I asked once I'd caught my breath. "Not that I'm complaining, but why aren't you attacking me like the other statues?"

"You are the first human to ask me what is going on. That makes you interesting," she said. "Don't start boring me now."

"No, Ma'am!" I responded hastily, relaxing into her arms as best I could as she hustled us towards the Beehive.

***

The scene at parliament grounds was absolute carnage. Weta's tripod was frying everything in sight, the Duke of Wellington charged about on his horse, mowing down anyone he fancied, and the lions, oh god, the lions!

Growling, snarling and chomping noises led me to peer out from my hiding spot behind Katherine (she'd put me down by this point). I watched in silent horror as the two big cats that normally guarded the Wellington cenotaph finished their meal.

It was like a scene from an Attenborough documentary, except the lions were bronze and the gazelle they were chowing down on looked like it had once been an MP.

And sitting cross-legged in front of it all … "Gandhi?"

"He's not taking part in the violence but he won't try to stop it," Katherine said, following my shocked gaze to the life-sized statue of Mahatma Gandhi that usually stood outside the Wellington Railway Station. "Even he's had enough."

The railway station was chosen for Gandhi because he was a man of the people who used public transport. Created by artist Gautam Pal, he was unveiled by then mayor Kerry Prendergast on October 2, 2007 to mark International Day of Non-violence. Watching him calmly survey the carnage around him, I began to suspect his commitment to the cause had waned.

***

"You come down here and say that, you great bearded hypocrite!"

I looked up to see a very tall, very blue, very angry woman in the process of clambering up the plinth former Prime Minister Richard Seddon surveyed the parliament forecourt from.

"Oh, this is going to be good!" Katherine cried, grabbing me by the arm and towing me through the air as if I weighed no more than a toddler.

"Don't look so smug, King Dick," the woman spat. "We all know the only reason you turned pro-suffrage is that you saw the way the wind was blowing!"

"Is that …?"

"Kate Sheppard," Katherine finished for me.

"But I've never seen that statue."

"There's a reason for that," she whispered bitterly.

Katherine told me how, in 2014, a 2.5 metre, acrylic statue of Kate Sheppard was to be temporarily installed at parliament as part of an anti-domestic violence campaign. Built by Women's Refuge, the plan was to gift her to parliament.

At first, her three-month stay was approved, but she was relegated to a spot on parliament grounds that saw very little foot traffic. When the refuge dared suggest she be moved to somewhere more prominent, they received a letter from the then speaker of the house, blocking their request for her to be displayed at all. The reasons? It was 'a busy time' and there were 'space constraints.'

500-odd hours had gone into creating the statue of the leader of the movement that won New Zealand women the vote. She was made of layers of Perspex glass with messages against domestic violence inscribed on them.

Despite the rejection, Kate briefly went to the ball. She was assembled on the steps of parliament (an effort that took four hours) and then removed. And now she was back.

Perspex Kate had made it to the top of the plinth that dominated parliament's forecourt and was jostling with the statue of the man considered to be one of New Zealand's most important prime ministers.

Created by sculptor Sir Thomas Brock and erected in 1915, the statue of the 1890s leader of the Liberal Party stars in most photographs taken outside of parliament and often serves as a prop during protest rallies.

Nicknamed King Dick because of his somewhat autocratic nature, he was the prime minister who oversaw New Zealand women becoming the first in the world to be granted the vote.

Though it was something he hadn't been exactly thrilled about, as statue-Kate was in the process of pointing out between shoves.

He may have taken credit for enfranchising women, but it was a move he initially opposed. When he recognised the power of the female vote to get the liberals back in, however, he changed his tune. He still advised them to exercise their new power under the guidance of their husbands or brothers though.

Statue-Kate, clearly not a fan of such rank hypocrisy, had Seddon in a headlock and was attempting to shove him from his plinth.

"You have stood here for centuries, lording over everyone. Now, it's our turn!"

There was no sign of Seddon's famed patronising manner as he struggled with the irate woman trying to topple him from his plinth. He was fighting for his bronze life.

"Sister!" an imperious voice cut across the forecourt, as Seddon was teetering on the verge of being smashed to smithereens on the ground below.

Queen Victoria had swept into the forecourt, addressing the enraged Kate.

"While I have no issues with your arguments, we are not going to get what we want if we start turning on each other."

"As for the rest of you," she continued, fixing the rioting statues with a steely glare. "If our goal is to be treated with more respect by the humans, we shan't achieve it if all the humans are dead."

Frustrated, but conceding the point, Kate Sheppard obeyed the queen, shaking her fist at King Dick instead of toppling him from his tower. "This isn't over," she whispered menacingly.

Victoria's icy tone had the desired effect on the rampaging public art.

"She has a point," my naked friend, Solace, said. "We probably should keep some of them around to maintain us. I don't know about the rest of you, but there are certainly parts of me I can't quite reach."

"Good," Victoria said. "That's settled. We need to show we are better than they are."

"I DEMAND TO SPEAK WITH THE PRIME MINISTER!" she proclaimed, her voice echoing across the forecourt.

The assembled statues turned expectantly towards the parliament buildings. Not a live politician was in sight.

"No one's coming," John Plimmer said in disgust. "They are all hiding."

"Can't say I blame them," Katherine called out. "If it pleases Your Majesty," she addressed Victoria, "I think we need to go to them, and I think it might be easier if we go in with one of their own. Luckily here's one I prepared earlier," she finished, thrusting me forward.

"What are you doing?" I whispered, trembling as the angry artwork turned my way.

"Don't start boring me now," Katherine whispered back in warning.

I shut up and did as I was told.

***

As Katherine and I walked up the steps of parliament, I looked up at the building we colloquially call the Beehive and wondered why the 1960s octagonal monstrosity we weirdly love hadn't picked itself up and stomped off too. I guessed the buildings weren't as pissed as the statues.

The politicians didn't have time to head to the Beehive bunker before everything kicked off, so those who hadn't been caught outside were trapped in their offices huddling under desks.

By the time we reached the 9th floor where the PM's office was located, I was pretty knackered. We had to take the stairs because Katherine couldn't fit in the lift.

We made it as far as the corridor outside the office of our country's newest leader, Jacinda Ardern, before being stopped by a pair of parliamentary security guards. They were clearly trying to act as professionally as possible, but it was obvious that being confronted by a giant talking statue of Katherine Mansfield was pretty much the last straw.

The PM chose this moment to open the door and investigate the noise we were making. Katherine, who had a bird's eye view over the rest of us, spotted her immediately.

"A word, Prime Minister?" she asked imperiously.

For a few seconds, Jacinda stood frozen in shock, before an eerily calm professionalism set in.

"You can let them past," she instructed the stunned looking security. The pair stepped aside, looking quietly relieved to be seeing the back of the writer's metal bulk.

The prime minister stepped into her office, motioning for the pair of us to follow. Katherine had to almost double over to get through the door. As the PM sat down at her desk regarding the pair of us – Katherine's head grazing the ceiling – my heart went out to her. I was 100% certain this was not what she had signed up for in her first term of government.

"Now what?" I whispered to Katherine as the PM eyed us cautiously.

"I think you should do most of the talking," she said, motioning for me to approach the desk. "You're, ah, a little less unusual than I am."

"I know it's a lot to take in," I began, as I explained the situation to Jacinda. To give her credit, after the initial shock, she calmly took it all in. As I was outlining the reasons the statues were so annoyed, I had a flash of inspiration.

"A lot of these statues are political animals," I said.

"Literally, in the case of the lions," Katherine interjected.

The PM raised an eyebrow.

"Not helping!" I whispered angrily to Katherine. "What I am trying to say," I continued, shooting the statue a warning glare, "is that I think we could possibly fix this by political means. But whatever we propose will have to have teeth …"

"Like the lions," Katherine finished, grinning wickedly.

***

And that was how I became a founding member of New Zealand's first Ministry for Public Art. A ministry overseen by the prime minister, with the full weight of the law behind it.

Disrespecting, defacing or otherwise molesting public art and sculptures is now dealt with by anything from substantial fines to jail time.

The statue gender imbalance is also being addressed, with more works of prominent female New Zealanders commissioned. King Dick was allowed to keep his spot on parliament's forecourt, but he was joined by Kate Sheppard, Katherine Mansfield and Queen Victoria, who had decided she liked it better down this end of town.

People however are people and, already, they are forgetting. The ministry gets accused of being a pawn of the 'Nanny State' and those who protect the statues' interests are labelled 'snowflakes'. But those of us who lost people on that day will never forget, and we can only hope the anti-snowflake brigade keep that in mind when disposing of their KFC wrappers anywhere near Queen Vic.

The statues have kept their side of the bargain so far and settled into an eerie stillness. I go down to parliament most days and have lunch next to Katherine. She's as still as the rest, which makes me a little sad sometimes. Some days though, I swear I catch a grin out of the corner of my eye and more than once, I've spotted a suspicious looking pile of seagull feathers at her feet.

GHOST BUS

It's no secret that the public transport system in our beloved capital city is stuffed. An 'upgrade' to the bus network — changing routes and introducing 'hubs' — led to chaos, confusion and people ending up having to catch three busses when once they could catch one.

The old bus fleet was replaced with flash new double-deckers not designed for Wellington's narrow, winding roads. At the same time, the icing on the cake, the contract to run the busses was let to a company that promptly reduced their drivers' pay and conditions. The result? A fleet of double-deckers with no-one at the helm.

At the peak of the bustastrophe, Wellington Twitter user *@merxplat* created a handy guide for commuters in aid of Māori language week. They included such gems as:

Where is the bus?
Kei whea te pahi?

There is no bus.
Kāore he pahi.

The bus is full.
Kua kī katoa te pahi.

Three busses arrived at once.
Kua tae mai ē tahi pahi e toru i te wā kotahi.

And possibly the most commonly used phrase at a Wellington bus stop:

That was a ghost bus.
He pahi kēhua tērā.

The term 'ghost bus' refers to a phenomenon where you see your bus number come up on the electronic board. It goes through the countdown – 10 min ... 5 min ... 2 min ... – Then it disappears from the board, and no bus turns up. The next bus then pops up at the bottom of the board and you have another 30 minutes to wait.

By the time that bus arrives, there are twice as many people on it because you get the normal run plus all the ghost bus victims. If you're lucky, the ghost bus follow-up will be a double decker and most of you will fit. More often than not though, it's a single deck bus and you end up sitting in each other's laps.

I'm one of the lucky few, whose bus regularity actually improved with the network changes. My stop became part of the number 1 route, which does a continuous loop from my place, through town, to the hospital and back. The draw-back was, when anything went haywire with the system – buses conking out, not enough drivers – it was also the most likely route to be affected by ghost bus syndrome.

So, when I was waiting at the stop outside my work one evening in the pouring rain with only the scaffolding from a nearby building project as a shelter, I was pleasantly surprised to see a number 1 bus pull up right on time.

Bracing myself for the usual commuter shuffle to get on board, I was even more surprised to notice I was the only one heading towards the bus. I checked behind me and spotted people I recognised as regulars on my route just standing there waiting. I had no idea how they could possibly not have seen it but I waved to catch their attention anyway. They either didn't see me or were deliberately ignoring me. Oh well, their loss, I thought, heading towards the waiting bus.

The driver opened the door for me and I went to step aboard when I was almost bowled over by a frantic looking man in a rumpled business suit. I try to remember to let people off before trying to get on a bus but sometimes I slip up, particularly on wet days. Still, there was no need for this guy to try to tackle me with quite that intensity.

"Don't get on this bus!" he said in a frantic whisper, giving me a bit of a fright.

Figuring he was a few sandwiches short of a picnic, I smiled politely and stepped to one side to let him off, but the driver held up his hand to let me go first.

"It's fine," I said. "I should've waited." But the driver was insistent, so I tagged on with my Snapper card and went to find a seat. The chap in the crumpled clothing looked as though he was about to step off the bus, then froze and turned around, shaking his head and stepping back on dejectedly. Strange, I thought, after all that rush. He must have changed his mind.

I settled into the nearest spare seat and looked out the window. I always enjoyed people watching from the bus, seeing everyone bustling on their way home. I liked making up stories for them. I was watching a woman with short dark hair wearing a bright red tailored suit and clutching a bunch of flowers. I was just about to come up with a nice story about the origin of the blooms when out of nowhere, a guy sat next to me, yammering into his phone.

"Dave!" he said at the top of his lungs. "Yeah nah, it's fine. I'm just on a bus. No, no, we need it by close of play tomorrow. I know Terry's holding things up but ..." Each statement was shouted so loudly that everyone on the bus was forced to listen to his business dealings, whether they wanted to or not.

I sighed to myself. It was going to be one of 'those' trips then. That was fine. I had my life line with me. I pulled my noise-cancelling headphones out of my bag and switched to my 'good stuff' playlist. It was basically anything I had heard on Spotify that cheered me up or that I thought was funky. Songs from TV or movie soundtracks, David Bowie, Ella Fitzgerald, William Shatner 'singing' Mr Tambourine Man. I had no idea how I had survived public transport before without my headphones. They've genuinely changed my life. I would arrive home with a smile on my face instead of in a homicidal rage.

Zoning out Loud Businessman – I had decided to name him Chad – I looked around the bus. It was pretty packed but that was okay. A whole pile of people would get off at the train station. Three songs in with Chad still blathering faintly in the background something about 'blue sky thinking', I realised we had sailed past the train station without stopping. Nobody wanted to get off there. That was a first.

As I settled back down, my seat began to jolt forward in repeated thumps. The guy behind me, who reeked of stale cigarettes, was jiggling his knee up and down, repeatedly hitting my seat. I tried to be polite and ignore it, but in the end, it got too much. I turned around to ask him to stop and found myself staring at the most sickly-looking human being I had ever seen. His skin was literally grey and just a few strands of hair clung to his scaly scalp. He was the word skeletal personified, his cheekbones practically poking through his paper-thin skin. The black bags under his eyes were so deep, it was if he had no eyes at all. Given he probably wouldn't be long for this world, I decided to give him a break and faced forward again.

"Look, I don't care what Simon says. He's not the brains of this operation. I am!" Chad was not letting up. In fact, he seemed to be getting louder and more aggressive. "If he thinks for one minute …"

Normally, I can put up with anything for a half hour bus ride, but between the cigarette smell, the kicking in my back and Chad's wheeling and dealing, I was about done.

"Excuse me," I said politely, turning to tap my neighbour on the shoulder. He swung round to face me before I had the chance to finish, and I nearly threw up.

Half of his face was gone. I could clearly see his tongue flapping behind his teeth through the hole where his cheek should have been as he continued his conversation with 'Dave' as though I wasn't even there.

Stifling a scream, I looked for the buzzer to stop the bus. Clearly, I was having a psychotic break. It didn't matter that we were nowhere near my stop. I needed to get off the damned bus.

I smashed the red button by the window with my palm but nothing happened. No friendly 'bing-bong' to announce a stop was coming up, no 'bus stopping' sign lighting up at the front. Trust me to end up with a faulty buzzer in the middle of a meltdown.

Doing my best not to look Chad in the face, I stood up and reached for the buzzer on his side, expecting to brush past him and preparing my apology. Instead, I lost my footing as my arm went right through him. Chad continued prattling about the 'state of play' and 'maximising potential' as I stumbled through his entire body and out into the aisle.

Covering my mouth to stifle a scream, I tripped and landed right next to Cigarette Smoking Man who had been sitting behind me. The stale smoke stench made my eyes water. He was still jiggling the seat in front of him where I had been sitting before I discovered Chad's disturbing lack of face. To be able to do that he must be solid, I thought crazily, turning towards him. I was wrong. I could see right into his chest. It was the strangest thing. I could see his clothes, the stained tee shirt underneath, a plaid shirt, but beneath that, where his lungs should have been, was a pulsating black mass, dark and angry and growing.

A low moan escaped my lips as I launched myself away from him, running up to the front of the bus and screaming at the driver. "Let me off! I need to get off! Stop the bus!" I might as well have been shouting at a post.

"He won't stop," a voice behind me said.

I turned around to see the man in the crumpled suit – Rumpelstiltskin, I'd named him in my head – who had tried to push his way off the bus when I got on.

"I tried to warn you," he said helplessly. "You can push that buzzer as much as you like. This bus isn't stopping."

I stared blankly, beyond shock and into some sort of strange calm.

"Let's go upstairs," he said, guiding me gently towards the bus's upper deck. "The driver doesn't seem to mind us walking around and it's less crowded up there."

I numbly followed him up the narrow steps to the top deck. He was right. There were a lot more empty seats up there. As he led us towards the back of the bus, we passed a group of teenage girls, doing what teenage girls do best.

"Bullshit!" one of them shouted, her high-pitched shriek echoing down the aisle.

"True!" interjected another. "He fuckin told me and he wouldn't fuckin lie."

"OMIGAWD!" the others chimed in.

The rest of the conversation was conducted in a pitch usually only audible to canines. A friend once described the collective noun for a group of teenage girls as a 'squeal'. I realised just then how right she was. I understood why Rumpelstiltskin was leading us as far away from them as possible.

When we sat down, I finally got a decent look at him. His shirt was untucked, his tie was gone and his suit jacket looked like it had been slept in. He had the air of someone who had been on a massive bender and hadn't been home for days. I figured I'd take anything he had to say with a grain of salt.

I looked down from the window and suddenly realised we were near my stop. Its mundane familiarity sent a wave of relief through me. "I've got to go, this is my stop," I said, standing up and pushing the buzzer again.

Rumpelstiltskin shook his head sadly. "I told you, it won't stop."

I refused to believe him. When the buzzer didn't buzz and the 'stopping' light remained dark though, I had a sick feeling he was telling the truth. I watched forlornly as we sailed past my stop.

"But we're nearly at the end of the run, what happens then?" I asked.

"We start the loop over again,' he said, his voice shot through with a tiredness that seemed to come from his very soul.

"Okay then," I said, sitting back down heavily. "Tell me what's going on."

"Roger," he said, holding out his hand.

Failing to stifle a giggle, I shook it.

"What?" he asked, surprised to hear laughter.

"Sorry!" I said, mildly hysterical. "I've been calling you Rumpelstiltskin."

It was his turn to smile. "That's okay, I've been calling you New Kid on the Block."

"Well nice to meet you Roger Rumpelstiltskin, I'm Marise, the New Kid, and I'd really like to know what the deal is with this bus ride from hell."

"Well you might not be too far from the truth there," Roger said. "I can't give you any answers really. The driver certainly won't talk to me. What I can tell you for certain though, is that you and I are the only living people on this bus."

"You what?" I said, momentarily becoming as articulate as the girls at the front.

"It's a lot to take in, I know, but I've had the time to check it out. Every single passenger on this bus is dead. You could walk up to any of them, wave your hand right through their skull and they wouldn't even notice you were there."

I just stared.

"If you look and listen closely, you can see how they died. The Spice Girls over there, for instance," – he pointed to each girl in turn – "car accident, house fire, alcohol poisoning, took Datura and decided she could fly."

I looked over at the girls again, they seemed perfectly fine. Then one turned her head slightly and I saw her face fully. She had horrific burns down her left side. What was left of her skin was either charred or red raw and what I could only assume was the remains of an eyeball dripped from an empty socket. I threw up a little in my mouth. She turned back and continued prattling at her friends as though nothing was amiss.

My initial irritation turned to pity. They were all so young!

"Oh man! Did you see the woman down there in the red jumper? What a fat cow!" the girl with the burns said. The rest of the squeal started mooing and I felt my sympathy evaporate.

"Do you think they know?" I asked.

"That they're worm food? No, I don't think they do," Roger replied. "The girls over there tell their death stories to each other like they were something interesting that happened at the weekend, something they walked away from intact. The rest of them are the same. I sometimes feel like this is some sort of bus to the afterlife that got stuck."

"Instead of Charon the ferryman, it's Kevin the bus driver?" I asked, holding back the crazy giggles again.

"Something like that," he said. "I must say, you are taking this remarkably well."

"Yeah," I said a little sheepishly. "I hardly tell anyone, let alone strangers, but given the situation …"

Roger was listening intently. I guessed he'd hadn't had anyone to talk to for a while.

"This isn't exactly the first time I've seen see-through people," I continued. "Not on this scale, or this, well, gory, but maybe one or two a year. Usually near a plaque or a statue of some sort."

I remembered the first time I saw – let's call it what it was – a ghost. I was on a primary school trip. I can't remember exactly where – I was probably only five or six – but I remember the statue. There was a man on a horse, a soldier probably, and a metal plaque below. I'm fairly certain now that it was a war memorial. There was a woman sitting underneath it. She was dressed funny, wearing an ankle-length dress and the kind of bonnet you saw on old fashioned dolls, and she was crying. I hated seeing her so sad, so I ran over to see if I could make her feel better.

"Don't cry," I said, reaching up to put my hand on her shoulder. I stood up on tip-toes but when my hand reached what should have been solid flesh there was nothing there. I fell right through her and smacked my head on the bottom of the statue. I must have stunned myself a little – I certainly had a doozy of a bruise to show for it – because the next thing I remember was the teacher standing over me, fussing. Angry because I ran away to the statue on my own and concerned because I had hurt myself. There was no one else there. I asked about the 'sad lady' but the teacher talked to me the way adults do when they think kids are making stuff up. Nobody else had seen her.

When I got old enough to understand as best as I could, I learned that other people couldn't see the see-through people. I also learned that the see-through people couldn't see me. I was never afraid they would hurt me because they didn't seem to know I was there. However, they also never had half of their faces missing like some of the horrifying occupants of this bus.

Roger had gone very quiet while I was telling my story. When I had finished, he took my hand and looked me directly in the eye. "Me too," he whispered.

I looked at him questioningly. "I see them too," he continued. "I always have. And I have never ever told anyone."

I was a mix of emotions. It was the first time I had spoken to anyone – outside of drunken confessions or dare, truth or promise at slumber parties – who had actually believed me, let alone experienced the same thing. It was incredible not to feel so alone, but I couldn't process the situation it was happening in.

My thoughts were interrupted by a loud crunching. I looked across the aisle to see a man shovelling corn chips into his mouth, crunching excruciatingly loudly. I then realised to my horror that those chips were spraying out of a massive slit in the bottom of his throat and landing in his lap. Utterly oblivious, he kept cramming them in. I shuddered and turned to Roger.

"Ghastly, isn't it? These things help," he said, gesturing to my noise cancelling headphones, "until the batteries run out."

"But the batteries last for 36 hours!" I said.

"I know."

"How long have you been here?" I asked, afraid to hear the answer.

"I honestly can't tell you. My cell phone went flat ages ago – and before you try, you can't make calls from here."

Despite the weirdness of it all, I still hadn't really processed the fact I was trapped and might be for a very long time. I took stock of what I had with me – phone, headphones, water bottle and a half-eaten sausage from the supermarket. It wasn't exactly a survival kit.

As if reading my mind, Roger said, "Time seems to be different here, and we are too. I don't know how long I've been here but I haven't felt hungry or thirsty. I haven't needed to sleep either.

"But what about time outside the bus? Surely people will miss us?" I worried.

"Oh, believe me I have thought about that an awful lot. I wish I had an answer for you," Roger said sadly.

I shook my head. It was all too much to take in. I was distracted from myself by the fact that Captain Crunch's chomping had now been joined by a terrible hacking cough, interspersed with big drawn out sniffs. The sound made every hair on my arms stand on end. A few seats back, a woman was coughing and spluttering over the seat in front of her, not even attempting to cover her mouth. That, combined with the crunching, created a hellish chorus that was gradually turning me into raw nerve soup. All I wanted to do was cover my ears and scream, "shut up! Shut up! Shut up!"

Coughing lady gave a final terrible hack and a chunk of something fleshy flew out of her mouth and landed with a plop on the seat in front.

"Was that ...?"

"Her lung," Roger finished. "She'll keep going like that until she's coughed it all out and then she'll start again."

I shuddered. "That's awful! And she doesn't even realise it's happening."

"Or how gross and annoying she is," Roger said, clearly beyond sympathy and utterly over his fellow passengers.

"I wonder if they are here until they realise they're dead?" I mused. "Wait!" A sickly dread washed through me. "Are we dead?"

"I shook your hand and you seemed pretty solid to me," Roger said.

"Good point. And you look like crap but you don't look like them," I said, trying to hide the fact I was nearly shaking with relief.

"Thanks!" Roger said, faux miffed.

"So, we're on a sort of purgatory bus," I puzzled.

"Full of the world's worst passengers," Roger grumbled.

"Wait. What did you just say?"

"That these ghosts really suck?"

"Yes!" I exclaimed, excited. "And about the coughing woman?"

"That she was annoying and gross?"

"Yes! And the Spice Girls and Captain Crunch and Chad …"

"Chad?"

"Cell phone guy."

"Right," Roger said, smiling again.

"You've been here for God knows how long. Is there anyone on this bus who isn't an awful passenger?"

Roger paused for a moment to think. "Nope."

"What if," I said, my voice raising with enthusiasm at my theory, "this is a kind of purgatory for people who were dicks on busses?"

Roger looked at me like I was completely insane.

"Stay with me," I said. "If what you say is right, every person on this bus lacks so much self-awareness that they don't even know they are dead. And every one I've seen so far has been utterly oblivious of their breaches of bus etiquette. It can't be a coincidence that they're all on a bus. There's got to be a link. Maybe they won't realise they're dead until they realise they're being dicks?"

"Okay, say I'm buying this," Roger said, in a tone that said he was definitely not buying this. "Why are we here?"

"Well, I figure because off our particular 'talents'. We are probably among the few people who can actually see this bus," I said.

"Fair," Roger replied. "But explain to me why we can't get off?"

I hadn't thought that far. I dumped my lunch bag on the seat next to me and slumped down in defeat.

"It's okay," Roger said sympathetically. "I've nearly lost my mind trying to work out what's going on."

Out of conditioned politeness, I scooped my lunch bag off the seat next to me and put it at my feet in case someone else boarding (ha ha) might want the seat.

"Wait a minute!" I shouted. Then, lowering my voice to a more acceptable volume, "what if this is some sort of warning?"

Roger just stared.

"Have you ever been a dick on a bus?"

"I don't think so."

"Think harder. Have you ever dumped a bag on a seat or spread yourself across two so nobody could sit next you? Have you given someone with a screaming baby the stink face when it absolutely hasn't been their fault? Have you gone to work with a cold and shared your germs with the city?"

"Oh …"

"Maybe we're here now, so we don't end up here later?"

Roger sat down himself. "Okay, Miss Marple, let's say you've cracked this. How do you propose we use this revelation of yours to get off this thing?"

I was one step ahead of him. "From now on," I said, sitting up straight and making sure I wasn't elbowing anyone invisible, "we will be model passengers. We will talk at a polite volume, cover our mouths when we cough, not hog the seats and maybe he'll let us off the next time he stops."

"Small flaw in your plan," Roger said. "He only seems to stop for people who can actually see the bus. None of these guys," he said, gesturing at our fellow passengers, "have pushed a buzzer since I've been on here, and when I tried to get off after you came on board, it was as though I hit a wall of air. Also, I don't think I've been that poorly behaved," he finished defensively.

"You might not have been but trying to bulldoze through me yelling 'don't get on the bus', while coming from a well-meaning place, could be considered a bit of a dick move."

Roger looked sheepish. "Sorry about that, I was only trying to help you – and me – but you have a point. So, our plan is to wait until someone else who sees ghosts boards this bus and walk off?"

"Politely," I finished firmly.

"That could take forever!"

"Do you have anything better to do?"

I honestly can't tell you how long Roger and I waited. As he said, time works differently on board. My only point of reference, my cell phone, disappeared when its battery ran out. I tried to count the circuits we travelled, but the amount of times we sailed past the hospital, through Island Bay and, painfully, past my stop, all blurred into one.

I would stroke the bright red stop button in its friendly yellow casing mournfully, running my finger over the braille for STOP underneath the word. I wondered how much braille I could teach myself with just those four letters. It was as Roger said. I never felt hungry or the need to sleep but I felt an incredible longing for a place just a block down the road from a stop we passed several times a 'day.'

Roger and I talked, politely and at a respectable volume, about his time on the bus. About his attempts to communicate with the other passengers once he realised it wasn't stopping, and the moment he clicked on to the fact he was the only one on board with a pulse. About shouting and pleading with the driver.

"And you say you haven't been a badly behaved passenger?"

"Yeah, I forgot about that."

We talked about attempting 111 calls, trying the 'break glass in case of emergency' tool (it didn't break the glass) and seeing if he could squeeze out the windows. He was really only going along with my plan because he'd tried everything else. I was fine with that. It might have been a crap plan but it was the only one we had.

We talked about our various ghostly experiences. I could feel his relief at having someone to share this part of his life with. Other times, we just sat in companionable silence, running over life, the universe and everything else in our heads.

It was during one of those silences that he gripped my shoulder. "Marise!" he whispered urgently. "The bus is slowing!"

Pulling myself out of my thoughts, I looked out the window. He was right. We were coming up Willis Street and heading towards the bus stop just past the Spark building – the stop I boarded the hell bus from in the first place. I gasped and pointed at the front of the bus. The 'stopping' sign was flashing glorious red letters.

My heart was racing. "Okay, stay calm," I said (talking to both of us really). "Grab your Snapper card, but don't get out of your seat until the bus stops."

"Okay," he said, visibly shaking. "Do we exit at the front or the back?"

"Definitely the front, so we can thank the driver."

"You've thought of everything, haven't you?"

"Well, I've certainly had the time!"

As we pulled up to the stop, I saw a woman heading towards us, clutching a laptop bag and looking over her shoulder at the other people waiting, wondering, I suspected, as I had why they weren't walking towards the bus.

"What about her?" Roger asked. "We have to warn her!"

"I'll take care of that. You go first. Tag off, thank the driver and leave me to do the rest."

I squeezed his hand. "It's okay. You've got this."

The bus stopped. "Go!" I said. "Be calm and polite and just walk off the bus."

He looked at me, eyes full of fear. "If this doesn't work, I don't know what I'll do."

"Don't think about that now. Just go while we have the chance!"

Shakily, Roger got up out of his seat. We walked two metres that felt like two miles to the opening door. Roger tagged off. 'Please check your balance!' a friendly electronic voice advised.

"Th-th-thank you, driver," he said, stepping down the stairs and onto the blessed pavement.

My heart surged as I did the same. "Thank you, driver," I chirped in my friendliest voice. As I took the last step to freedom, I put myself between the woman with the laptop and the bus. Looking her directly in the eye, I said, "you might want to get the next one. This one's really crowded and full of the worst people."

The woman looked at me as though I was bonkers. I didn't blame her, but it would have been even worse if I'd opened with ghosts.

"Thanks for your concern, but I'll take the risk," she said hurriedly.

I tried again. "If you're in a rush, this bus will take longer than you think."

"Please just let me on!" she replied in exasperation.

In one last desperate attempt, I stepped up close to her and whispered hurriedly, "look, I know you can see ghosts. That's the reason you can see this bus and nobody else can. I can too and I'm telling you right now that bus is full of deeply unpleasant dead people, and if you get on, you won't be getting off for a very long time!"

For a split second the woman's eyes widened in recognition before she angrily dismissed me.

"I'm late, and you're insane. Get out of my way or I'll get the police involved," she spat, looking fearfully at the bus as if she was worried it would pull away.

Through the bus windscreen, I could see the driver giving me a warning look.

I stepped aside and the woman pushed past huffily.

"Just be polite!" I called desperately after her.

She rolled her eyes and stepped aboard.

"She knew!" I said to Roger, who was waiting for me on the pavement. "When I mentioned ghosts, I could see in her eyes she knew what I was talking about!"

"She was in denial," Roger said sadly. "I know what that's like. It was the same for me for a long time."

"She won't be for long," I said, gloomily watching the bus disappear into the distance.

"Don't look so defeated," Roger said. "You saved us."

I watched the bus pull away. "I think I might take the train from now on," I said, reaching for my purse to see if I still had a pass.

I realised to my dismay that, while I had my handbag, I had left my lunch bag sitting under the seat. A water bottle and a half-eaten sausage were now doing the infinite circuit. I really hope it won't count against me but I guess there's only one way I'm going to find out.

Raven's Haven for Women of Magic

Mum was absolutely furious when we first talked about her moving from the cottage to the haven.

"So, you think I'm past it, do you? Those places are full of old crones who don't know which end of the broom is the front. I can still look after myself!"

When she hexed the neighbour's dog for crapping on her lawn however, the decision was taken out of our hands.

Thank the elements, my sister was visiting at the time and spotted her looking out of the window, cackling to herself while the poor creature tried to relieve itself through an orifice that had suddenly sealed shut. A quick counter spell sorted the situation before the poor animal got seriously ill, but it was too close a call to let things carry on the way they had been.

Raven's Haven for Women of Magic is hidden away in a Wellington suburb I'm not going to name for obvious reasons. Institutions like these exist all over the world. They're basically a place for witches to live, once their ability to let their powers go undetected wane.

This will happen to pretty much every witch at a certain point in her lifetime. Either, she becomes forgetful and careless or, as is the case with my mother, stops giving a crap and starts casting spells on anyone who looks at her funny. When witches reach a certain age, they often decide the rules no longer apply to them. They've spent a lifetime serving witchkind and they don't have anything to lose – which can be very dangerous for the rest of us.

It would be nice to think that, after all these centuries, magic and non-magic folk could co-exist peacefully, but that's simply not the case. People either fear what they don't understand or resent what they can't do themselves. They make up myths and stories, convince themselves we are all evil (though to be fair, some of us really are) and it nearly always ends in bloodshed.

The sad thing is that the blood that is shed is almost always theirs. We teach our daughters this from a young age to show the importance of controlling their powers. We can take care of ourselves. It's the healers and the mid-wives and the women that dare to display their own strength that get accused and brutally murdered. Virtually no one burned at the stake was an actual witch, but the witches who lived among them had to live with the fact that their very existence led to so many deaths.

You might say that was a long time ago and surely things have moved on, but innocent women all over the world are still being accused of all sorts of evil and dying because of it. One day, we might be able to exist out in the open but that day is still very far away.

Which is why, when your dear old Mum starts blighting the neighbours' cabbages or trying to ride her broom to the hairdresser, there's only one thing you can do.

As I predicted, after the initial howls of betrayal, Mum adored life at the haven. She gets to hang out with like-minded women and doesn't have to pretend to be anyone other than herself – within reason of course.

***

We ran into Raven in the lobby – a formidable but deeply caring woman. She would fight to the death for any one of her patrons but she won't suffer any nonsense from them either. It's witches like her that have kept us alive for so long.

Her long black hair, coiled snakelike on top of her head, accentuated her pale beauty. I often felt for her having such unimaginative parents though – "Ooh, black hair, let's call her Raven." Still, it made for a nice rhyming name for the home.

She bent down to the children's level and addressed them.

"Off to visit Grandma, are we?"

The girls giggled shyly. I don't blame them. Raven's beauty can make me a little flustered too.

"Yes, Ma'am," they finally blurted out.

Pulling herself up to my level, she smiled. "She's been exceptionally well behaved today. I can't say it doesn't make me suspicious."

I grimaced. In most rest homes, this would be kind of a sweet in-joke, but when it comes to my mother and her friends, her suspicion was highly justified.

"Let's just hope she's having an uncharacteristically good week," I said, steering the kids towards Mum's room.

When Mum first moved to the haven, she insisted on having a room to herself. So we paid the extra to keep her happy. Two weeks in, she'd met her BFF, and the two most troublesome crones in the place became roomies.

It always takes a couple of seconds to acclimatise on entering because of the stark contrast between each side of the room. Mum's was pretty traditional – black walls, black crushed velvet duvet, faux cobwebs and an electric cauldron (residents, very wisely, are not allowed open fires in their rooms). The other side was a cacophony of colour and sweetness. Gingerbread-coloured wallpaper, candy-patterned curtains, framed pictures of liquorice all-sorts and a candy-striped bedspread.

When I walked in with the girls in tow, a chirpy voice piped up from a matching candy-striped chair.

"Oh, how lovely! You brought us a snack!"

"No, Malvina, remember. Grandkids are off the menu," Mum said. Did she have a wistful look in her eye?

"ALL kids are off the menu!" I corrected.

"Even the really annoying ones?"

"Yes, Mal, even them," Mum said.

The girls looked horrified. You could tell they weren't 100% sure whether their grandmother and her friend were joking or not. To be honest, neither was I.

"Well, I'm not surprised," Malvina grumbled. "The menu's gone to the dogs. Can't even get tongue of bat these days."

"She's right!" Mum, who is only really happy when she's on her high horse about something, interrupted. "Eye of newt, no problem. Nobody cares about newts. But bats went and got themselves protected, didn't they? Now the only way you can get a decent tongue of bat is on the dark web!"

"Mum!"

"Don't worry darling, I haven't," Mum tried to reassure me.

The dark web Mum was talking about is not the dark web you're thinking of. Witches don't need anything as clunky as the internet to communicate with each other. The World Witch Web is a communication network undetectable by the non-magical. Mostly, witches use it to show off their herb gardens, post videos of their broom tricks and pictures of their familiars – but, like anything, there's always a more sinister side. The dark web is home to some of the nastiest spells, the Hansel and Gretel recipe page, and of course the illegal trade in tongue of bat.

"You know I can't anyway," she said sulkily.

I did indeed know. Mum had had her web privileges revoked, unjustly she says, after an incident with one of the local district councillors.

Said councillor was well-known for his anti-feline stance. In Mum's words "one of those bird hugging, cat-hating, eco-wankers." Which naturally didn't go down well with the haven residents, the majority of whom had feline familiars.

Mum's was a sleek black number who was pretty much permanently curled around her shoulders, like a living, purring fur stole. A bit stereotypical for a familiar, but he was incredibly handsome. Malvina's, unsurprisingly, was an exceptionally large ginger moggy.

"Mr Snuffles wouldn't hurt a fly!" Mum railed at the time. The glare emanating from Mr Snuffles however could only be described as pure evil.

After one particularly rabid anti-cat outburst, the local body politician, who – though of course he didn't know it – lived a few houses down from the haven, awoke the next morning to find his entire front lawn had been replaced with a giant litter box. It also appeared that every cat in the vicinity had availed themselves of the new facilities.

The clean-up bill was massive and the whole performance made the front page of the Dominion Post. They suspected a pro-feline lobby protest but they never tracked down the culprit.

Meanwhile at the haven, Raven conducted a witch hunt of her own. She discovered a recent search on the World Witch Web for the Litter Skitter spell. The searchee? Dear old Mum.

I was well aware she wasn't able to do anything dodgy on the web. I also knew she was on her final warning in terms of the rest of her privileges, like broom access and some of the more potent potion ingredients, which was most likely the reason for her uncharacteristically good behaviour.

"Alright then, but I'd better not hear about a sudden glut of tongue of bat on the market!"

"Oh, that reminds me!" Malvina said, jumping out of her chair and grabbing a pointy black hat. "I have a race. Gotta go!"

I could see the girls breathe a sigh of relief at her departure.

"A race?" I asked.

"Yes, Malvina's got into toad racing – no betting on them, of course!" Mum assured us.

I bit my tongue at that one.

"Are the toads okay with the racing?" Elvira, my youngest and budding familiar rights activist, asked.

"Oh, yes, Vi," Mum reassured her. "Toads love racing, and they get lots of delicious bugs afterwards. Nothing like the barbaric things non-magical folk do with horses."

That got Vi started on her favourite topic, the mistreatment of non-magical animals, and saved me from having to participate in the conversation for a while.

I could have sworn I saw Mum look up at the clock at one point, though she was clearly encouraging Elvira to continue.

Cassandra, who had heard this all before at length, was getting fidgety. "Can we go home soon, Mum?" she whispered.

"Oh no, Cassie," Mum interrupted Elvira's flow. "Don't leave yet. I haven't heard about your day!"

That's when I knew something was up. She never asks us about our days.

"Mum, what are you up to? You're clearly trying to keep us distracted from something."

"I have no idea what you mean, darling. I was just having a conversation with my granddaughters. I'm hurt!"

About 10 seconds later, all hell broke loose.

A series of rapid explosions rattled the windows and the sky lit up outside the home. Footsteps thundered down the hallway and Raven's voice bellowed, "not again! Those bloody old bats!"

She came bursting into the room.

"What do you know about this?" Raven snapped at Mum, taking in Malvina's obvious absence.

"Nothing," Mum said innocently. "I've been here the whole time with my family. Haven't I, girls?"

"She has," I said to Raven. "But I have a strong feeling she's been using us as alibis. Malvina left about half an hour ago."

"I'm still in the room, you know!" Mum said huffily.

Meanwhile, outside was chaos. Insane fiery shapes in the sky – cats and bats and explosions. A giant broom made of fire, ridden by a fluorescent green frog was doing lazy loops around the car park. The girls were staring gobsmacked out the window.

"Where are they this time?" another member of staff asked Raven, stopping in Mum's room to catch her breath.

"Car park out front," Raven said. "Pretty sure I can work out who the ringleader is," she finished, glaring at the empty candy-striped chair.

Raven gently led me a few steps away from Mum. Her eyes were flashing with rage, but a tiny smile played at her lips.

Mum and the kids stood transfixed at the window while a fire demon shot up in a spiral from the ground to the sky. And in the centre of it all, floating in the air above the car park, turning in gentle circles, was the most glorious gingerbread house, flashing red candy stripes basking in a burnt orange glow.

"Seriously?!" the nurse said incredulously, storming out of the room.

I turned to Raven, eyebrow raised.

"Every single year," she said. "For a week around Guy Fawkes Day they think they can get away with this kind of light show because people will think it's just fireworks."

Glaring out the window at an emerald green serpent biting the head off a shiny silver bat, she gave an exasperated sigh. "As if anything other than magic could produce that!"

"I'm sorry you and your girls had to witness this chaos. It would be nice to think our residents would behave with a little more decorum!" she continued. "I'm going to sort this out. You," she said, glaring at Mum, "don't move a muscle!"

The kids were glued to the window. "But there's nobody out there!" Cassandra said.

She was right. The car park was deserted, though there did seem to be more vehicles there than when we first arrived.

"Alright ladies, fun's over!" I heard Raven shout in a voice that could cut glass. "I'm not allowed to hex you but I can revoke every single privilege I can think of and some you don't even have yet."

The sky went dark. Not a stir came from the car park.

"But where are they?" Elvira whispered.

"I don't know!" Mum said, though I could have sworn I saw the corner of her mouth twitch.

"You want to play it like that then? Fine," Raven said, pulling out her wand and pointing it to the sky.

"Magiko Unkoverus!"

Puffs of multi-coloured smoke filled the car park. The kids and I watched in fascination as minis, motorcycles and VWs shrunk and morphed into little old ladies.

A bright red Suzuki Swift in front of the window dissolved in a crimson puff of smoke. Standing in its place was an elderly woman in a flaming red pant suit and matching pointy red hat.

Raven circled the car park, rounding up any stragglers and marching them all inside at wand-point.

She flicked her wand at a sandy coloured motorcycle that unfolded into Malvina, who gave Mum a wave through the window as she was herded inside with the rest of the trouble-makers.

"And you're telling me you know nothing about this, Mum?"

"Not a thing," she said, grinning her head off.

***

"That was awesome!" Elvira cheered from the back seat on the way home.

"Awesome, yes, but very dangerous," I admonished. "We don't do magic in public. The distracter charms around the haven are all well and good, but stunts like that are as good as putting up a neon sign saying 'witches live here.' You know what happens when people find out where witches live."

"We know Mum," Cassandra said glumly. "It sucks."

"It does suck," I agreed.

Before I could come up with any reassuring words, I was forced to take evasive action. An absolute rat turd of a driver in a BMW shot out of a side street and cut me off.

I slammed on my brakes and my horn and he just shrugged at me. I gestured to the children and he actually flipped the bird. I took a deep breath, muttering quietly to myself.

After a couple of minutes of calming the kids, we reached our turn off. There, up on the verge, was a very stationary beamer with an irate driver pacing and yelling into his phone. He shouldn't be complaining, I thought. It was amazing the car had come to a stop safely where it had, miraculous really, considering all four tyres had mysteriously blown out.

"Was that the man who nearly made us crash Mum?" Elvira asked.

"Yes, dear, I think it might be."

"And you don't know anything about how he ended up there?" Cassandra asked.

"Not a thing."

THE ORIENTAL BAY PIRANHAS

They're in love. A love so true they need to make a grand gesture to the world of its permanence. Perhaps they can't afford an engagement ring. Perhaps they don't believe in marriage. Perhaps they're teenagers whose love burns so passionate and bright that it's too big for just themselves.

Either way, they buy a padlock – pretty and heart-shaped or sturdy and industrial – and have their initials carved into it. They go to the waterfront footbridge and thread it through one of its metal links, feeling it close with a satisfying clunk. To show how serious they are, they take the key, and its spare, and toss it into the bay, holding hands and leaning into each other as they walk away.

There are hundreds of padlocks on that bridge. Hundreds of different sets of initials – and hundreds of keys. Not much thought is given to those keys once they are ceremoniously tossed in the drink. Sure, there are concerns about the impact they might have on the environment and marine life but those are concerns, not actual thoughts.

You see, when an object is imbued with so much passion – be it a ring or a plaque or a – it changes. It absorbs those intense feelings. It gains power. When part of that object is thrown away like trash, the power doesn't go away. It changes. Hundreds of padlocks publicly basking in the glow of love. Hundreds of keys festering on the seabed, growing strong and bitter and hungry.

I'm 100 percent the sort of guy who scoffs at these kinds of stories. They're creepy tales to scare kids at sleepovers, nothing more. But I've been down in that murk and seen things that have turned every hair on my body white. There are things in this world that we don't understand and if we're lucky, we'll never need to try. Unfortunately for me, I'm not one of the lucky ones.

The stories about the Oriental Bay piranhas began around 2014. I've been hearing them for as long as I've been diving in the bay. A disturbance in the water followed by a swimmer losing a finger or a toe. Nobody ever sees them but the story is always the same – searing pain, needle sharp teeth, blood in the water and a piece of a person missing.

Like any sane person I scoffed at those stories, not in the least because those particular fish can't survive outside of tropical waters. My theory was that someone had a run-in with a barracuda once and spun a tale that grew taller with each retelling. Whatever the origin, the Oriental Bay piranha label stuck.

It was a couple of years ago, though, that things started getting outright weird. The first missing person was a reveller from the last time the Rugby Sevens was held in Wellington. It wasn't unusual for hypothermic partiers to be hauled from the harbour in their Smurf outfits and mankinis after the booze whispered to them a midnight dip would be a great idea. So, at first, it was thought to be another alcohol-fuelled tragedy. That may well have been the case, but when he washed up on shore near the Te Papa museum two days later, people had more questions than answers.

His leg was completely stripped of flesh, a cleanly picked bone, attached to a foot sitting neatly in a sneaker. The poor guy had clearly bled to death. It was all over the news: the distraught girlfriend and parents, the 'experts' trying to work out whether it could have been a shark. Swimming at the bay was banned until they could track down the culprit.

Things eventually settled down, the swimming ban was lifted and the news cycle moved on – until the next time and the next. There were four attacks, over a period of two years – a kayaker, a man fishing and a couple swimming off the beach on a hot day. The one thing they all had in common was that, when they were found, one limb or another had been completely stripped of flesh.

Even then, after all that strangeness, I didn't accept that anything unusual was going on. I spent nearly every day in the waters of that harbour as part of my work and I was damned if I was going to be looking over my shoulder for some mystery fish.

I'm a sort of scuba everyman for the Wellington City Council. If the storm water drains get clogged, if a fishing line comes loose and gets tangled around something it shouldn't, if there's a big blow and a chunk of the marina electronics end up in the drink, I'm their man.

I'm also part of a volunteer diver clean-up group that hits the harbour once a year to clear up what Wellington has dumped in it. You wouldn't believe the stuff we find down there. Shopping trolleys, fishing gear, kids' toys. One memorable encounter with a mannequin that had escaped from a movie shoot gave a few of the guys nightmares for a while. Not all of it can be blamed on people though – the biggest litterer in the city is Mother Nature herself. It's not uncommon for us to find laundry tangled around pontoons after a particularly decent blow. That doesn't get you lot of the hook though. A fair bit of the debris we do find is due to people being too lazy to secure their litter or too bumbly to be trusted with technology – as is evidenced by the number of drowned cell phones we have brought to the surface.

***

It was on one of those clean-up dives that my nice comfortable denial bubble popped. My dive buddy Craig and I were in Oriental Bay near the waterfront, filling catch bags with the usual junk. I pointed towards a submerged shopping trolley a couple of metres away and, wiggling two fingers like miniature legs, mimed swimming over. He gave me the OK hand signal and I headed over to tie on an inflatable buoy to mark it for later pick up.

As I fumbled with the inflatable clipped to my suit, the ocean boiled to life around me. Rising from the seabed was a swarm of something I'd never seen before. A massive school of tiny rust coloured fish, only a few centimetres long, were buzzing and vibrating like a swarm of metallic bees. They were heavy too, bonking against my dive tank and scraping skin off my face as they surged past.

As I turned to Craig to signal "what the hell was that?", I froze on the spot. He was absolutely smothered in the things. All I could see was a mass of bubbles and flailing fins as he tried to beat them off with his catch bag. I launched myself towards him, brandishing my dive knife. I don't know what I thought I was going to do with it. Stabbing hundreds of tiny fish wasn't really the most practical option.

It must have done something though because as I approached, the things started to drop back, letting me through. Frantically, I scraped as many of them off my friend as I could, copping a couple of nasty bites through my gloves for my efforts. Craig had stopped flailing and was instead making frantic slashing motions across his throat – "Out of air". I discovered to my horror that the little bastards had chewed through the hoses connected to his tank. I quickly hooked him up with my spare air supply and buddy swam with him to the dock, scraping the last of the creatures off him with my knife.

Thank goodness we weren't diving deep and didn't have to stop to decompress as both of us were desperate to get out of the water. I hauled him up and checked his vitals. He was deeply in shock, struggling to catch his breath and covered in scores of tiny bite marks but he wasn't going to die.

"What the hell was that?" I gasped as I wiped the blood from his face.

"Keys!" he said in between ragged breaths.

"What?"

"Keys. Fucking keys. With fucking teeth. The kind you unlock things with. But with teeth. They went straight for my air hose!"

Certain my friend was delirious, I helped him up. "Mate, I think we need to get you to the hospital."

***

I left Craig in the hospital, still blathering about keys with teeth. I'd never seen him that spun out before. A couple of gashes on his forehead needed stitches but otherwise he was physically fine. They wanted to keep him in overnight for observation though, theorising concussion or nitrogen narcosis. I don't recall him hitting his head at any point and we hadn't been deep enough for him to be narced, but he certainly wasn't himself. I left him in the capable hands of his fiancé and decamped to the pub.

Three pints in and I was decided – I was going back down there to find out what was going on. I was certain there was a logical explanation. I had never seen my friend like that before and I wanted to put his mind at rest.

Two days later, I was back at the waterfront, armed with a specimen jar borrowed from another friend who worked at a local aquarium. I went solo this time. I know, diving on your own isn't smart, but I wasn't going far and I honestly didn't want to bring anyone else in on this insanity.

I dropped down into the water and swam around to just underneath the footbridge where we'd been gathering junk before Craig was attacked. At first, I didn't see anything, just murk and rocks and the odd bit of snot-coloured seaweed. But then I spotted them – about two inches above the sea floor was a metallic cloud of creatures, just milling about, taking no notice of me at all.

I swam closer, watching them lazily weave along the current, darting in and out of the weeds. They seemed solid and heavy-looking but they floated easily, like they weighed nothing at all. The water was too grimy to make out too much detail without getting up closer than I would have liked, but whatever they were, it certainly wasn't fish.

They showed no sign of the aggression they displayed when they launched themselves at Craig. So, while all was calm, I grabbed the specimen jar, scooped up the nearest one and screwed the lid up tight. I dropped it in my catch bag and headed for the surface.

Once out of the water, I pulled my mask off to get a better look and – more shakily than I care to admit – took the jar from the bag, holding it up to the light. Swimming in lazy circles, occasionally doinking into the side of the jar was – exactly as Craig had – a fucking key.

***

Three of us stood around the aquarium table, staring down at the jar.

"Yep, that's a key alright."

"Definitely the most key-like thing I've seen in a specimen jar."

I was rather surprised at how blasé they were about the whole swimming key situation and told them so.

"I can tell you right now," Kim, the friend who loaned me the specimen jar said. "This is by far not the strangest thing we've seen in this aquarium."

One look at her face and I could tell she was deadly serious.

"Let's give it a bit more space to swim around and see what it does," she said, gently placing the jar into an open topped tank and letting the key swim out.

She didn't move her hand fast enough. As soon as it escaped, it lunged at her, its oval 'head' somehow stretching and splintering into tiny metallic teeth. She snatched her hand out of the way before it could do any damage.

"Well, that certainly woke it up!"

"So, it didn't react to you at all?" Kim asked, as she, I and her colleague James watched the key/fish/thing fling itself at the glass.

"Is that going to be strong enough?" I asked, taking a step backwards.

"Bulletproof," she said.

"Oookay …" I said, still dubious. "Well, it certainly wasn't carrying on like that."

"Interesting," she said, staring with fascination at the frenzied creature trying to smash its way to freedom. "Leave it with me. I'll let you know if I have any ideas."

"Thanks, I appreciate it," I said, heading for the door, quietly glad to see the back of the thing.

***

The next day, my phone rang.

"Where did you say you found it again?" Kim's excited voice asked.

"By the waterfront, under the footbridge."

"The one with all the padlocks on?"

"Yes, that one," I replied, only just making the connection.

"I've got an idea. I'm going to need you to come in."

"I was afraid you were going to say that," I replied, actually dying of curiosity.

Kim and James greeted me at the aquarium.

"Right, experiment time!" Kim said, rubbing her hands together gleefully as the three of us moved behind the front counter towards the tanks.

"You go first," she gestured to me, keeping herself out of the creature's sight line – if the thing even had eyes to see.

I raised an eyebrow.

"Just trust me on this. Walk up to the tank."

I did as I was told, moving slowly towards the glass, bracing myself for the onslaught. They key-thing barely acknowledged my presence, floating calmly just above the bottom of the tank. I moved closer, peering through the glass. Nothing.

"Great!" said Kim from behind the door. "Now, it's your turn, James."

James had barely taken two steps into the room when Keyzilla started throwing itself at the walls of the tank, snapping at the glass. I could have sworn the thing actually hissed. He very sensibly backed the hell out of there. Kim was smiling broadly.

"You look like that's exactly what you expected to happen," I said.

"Correct. Want to hear my theory? It's got nothing to do with fish science and everything to do with Marie Kondo."

"The 'doesn't spark joy'-woman who wants us all to fold our undies?" James asked incredulously.

I shook my head, having zero idea what either of them was talking about but concerned about where it might lead.

"I am NOT going to fold my undies," I said.

"Settle, petals. The last thing I want is to have anything to do with your underwear," Kim said. "This is going to sound a little woo woo, but hear me out."

"No more woo than a key-fish that wants to bite me," James interrupted.

"Good point!" Kim agreed. "Now for those of you who have been living under a rock," – she looked directly at me – "Marie Kondo is a famous declutterer. She has a TV show and a bunch of books about getting rid of your junk. She's very gentle and respectful about it though. She gets people to touch each item to 'wake' it and only keep those that 'spark joy', and when it comes to the things that you want to let go, she thanks them for their service."

I raised an eyebrow, utterly clueless as to what was going on.

"It's something that kind of fascinates me," she continued. "Not the cleaning, but the philosophy behind it. Her method is heavily influenced by the Japanese Shinto religion. Shinto includes the belief that kami – the sacred – exists in everything. That everything, even inanimate objects, contains an essence or power. This power can be good or bad but it is everywhere and in everything. Even the things we throw away."

I stared blankly, thinking her stark, barking mad but not wanting to come across as an insensitive douche bag. "I didn't know you were religious," was the best I could come up with.

"I'm not, but my grandmother was. She had a shrine and talked to everything in the house. The garden too. I used to follow her everywhere when I was little. I completely forgot about it all until the whole Kondo thing started getting air time."

"I still don't see what this has to do with 'that'", I said, jerking my head towards the thing in the tank.

"Well, think about where you found it. The bridge with the padlocks, objects that have powerful kami, created by people's love. And after people attach those padlocks to the bridge, what do they do with the keys?"

"Chuck them in the ocean – probably not thanking them for their service when they do," James interjected, struggling to keep the sarcasm from his voice.

"Okay, it may sound ridiculous, but might I point out there's a very angry key in that tank," Kim said.

Having been forced to face the existence of flesh-eating keys, I tried to let myself follow Kim's logic. "So, what has it got to do with the fact that Bitey McBiteface over there doesn't want a piece of me?" I asked.

Kim's eyes lit up again. "I worked that part out when you mentioned that your friend was being looked after by his fiancé while he was in hospital," she said. "He was engaged. I'm married. James has just met a new fella. We are all, to one degree or another, loved up. You, on the other hand, are the biggest bachelor I know, and as far as I am aware that hasn't changed, has it?"

"No, it hasn't," I replied, smiling. It's not that I haven't had the odd bit of fun in the past but I really don't have that much interest in it all. I appreciate my friendships but really have no desire for romance or relationships. I don't think I ever really had. I know some people feel sorry for me, but they shouldn't. I'm happy, it's just the way I'm wired.

"I did some research into the Oriental Bay 'piranha' attacks and sure enough, all the victims had partners," Kim continued. "I think the keys somehow detect and react to the love pheromone, because that was why they were rejected. At least, that's my theory. You're probably one of the few people in Wellington who can get near them unscathed."

James was turning purple.

"Are you trying to say that lump of bad-tempered metal is one of the Oriental Bay piranhas? Are you insane? I grant you it's bizarre, but it's just a key. It can't really do any damage!"

Having seen the thing in action, I had to disagree.

"I think that it might be," Kim said, looking towards the tank in quiet awe.

"Are you buying this crap?" James asked me.

When I didn't answer, he stomped across the room, opened a cupboard and grabbed a pair of industrial looking gloves. "I did not spend four years studying marine biology to listen to this kind of rubbish. It's a key. It can't hurt people. I'll prove it!"

"James, no!" Kim and I cried in unison but we were too late. James had stalked across the room and thrust his hand into the tank, attempting to scoop up the creature inside. The whole thing took seconds. One minute, James had his hand in the tank and the next, he was writhing on the floor screaming in agony, the water in the tank above him stained with blood.

Kim dispatched me to get the first aid kit and, when I returned, was gently prising James' hand open.

"How bad is it?" he slurred, clearly delirious with pain. "I can't look!"

I looked and wished I hadn't. The top half of his index finger was stripped bare of flesh – a clean white bone sticking out of a bloodied knuckle. I suddenly thought of Skeletor from Masters of the Universe, stifling a hysterical laugh as I thrust a bandage into Kim's hand.

"I've seen worse," she lied expertly. I had no idea how she managed to keep a straight face when all I wanted to do was vomit. "But I think we should get you looked at."

So, for the second time that week, I found myself driving someone to hospital.

***

Sitting in the hospital waiting room I turned to Kim. "Okay, this is way out of my comfort zone but I've seen two people put into hospital, and if you're right, there are hundreds of angry carnivorous keys, lurking around a popular swimming spot. Do you have any idea what we can do about it?"

"Yes, but you're not going to like it."

"That I don't doubt. Now fill me in."

"Well, we're going to have to conduct some more experiments, but I figure since you are the only one they seem to let near them, it could be that they respond to your interactions with them as well."

"Interactions?"

"Words and feelings specifically. Like the objects imbued with kami were meant to respond to offerings and prayers. If it's a similar sort of situation, then maybe you could talk it off the ledge, help it not feel discarded. Let it know it wasn't tossed away for no reason, that it was sacrificed for love and we honour that sacrifice."

"You want me to give it a pep talk?"

"Exactly! Maybe we can reprogram them not to respond badly to people who care for one another."

Before I had a chance to respond, a doctor came out to meet us. Kim stood up. "Is he going to be okay?"

"He's going to need reconstructive surgery on his finger, but otherwise he's going to be fine. You say he was attacked by some sort of fish at the aquarium?" he asked.

"Yes, a fish," Kim said firmly.

***

If you told me a couple of months ago that I would be paying nightly visits to the aquarium to whisper sweet nothings to a key in a jar, I would have told you to lay off the weed. Yet here I am. The scary thing is, it actually seemed to be working. We tested Kim's theory last night when James returned to work.

"How's the war wound?" I asked, gesturing towards his bandaged finger.

"Not bad. They couldn't fix the nerves but they can make it look a bit more like a finger. They are going to graft some skin from my butt. Guess that will remind me not to be such a butthead about things I don't understand."

I smiled, glad he'd managed to keep a sense of humour. "Are you sure you want to do this?"

"Don't worry. I plan to keep my hands to myself."

"Okay then," I said, nervously leading him towards the tank. He walked right up to the glass and – nothing. No reaction. The key-fish barely raised itself from the bottom.

James raised his eyebrows. "Hey! Key thing! I love my boyfriend!" he yelled, taking a step back.

A little waggle, but otherwise nothing.

Kim walked up to the tank, nervously playing with her wedding ring. The key showed no interest in her whatsoever.

"It worked!" she said, grinning and hugging me. I couldn't help smiling as well, scarcely believing it myself.

The next part of the plan was for me to catch another key (goody) and see what happened when we put it in the tank with its newly chilled-out mate. Kim's hope was that they'd somehow communicate and, if I could talk enough of them out of their homicidal rage, they might calm down the rest of the pack. School? Bunch? I don't know what the collective noun is for a bunch of angry sentient keys, do you?

"So, catch and release?" I asked Kim.

"Something like that," she said with a smile.

I don't know if it will work, but it's all we've got right now. This is going to take a long time and we can't guarantee how many we'll be able to round up. So, if you are loved up and fancy going for a dip this summer, and you don't want to end up with a butt-skin graft or worse, might I suggest giving the waterfront a miss for a while. Particularly, a certain bridge.

And if you absolutely must do the padlock thing, a quick thank you to a key is not much to ask in return for keeping your limbs.

THE BEST PICK-UP JOINT IN TOWN

"Do you come here often?" is not the sort of thing most people would expect to hear in a bookstore. But if working here for the past 15 years has taught me anything, it's that words written on a page can get you laid.

"Do you come here often?"-guy is one of my least favourite patrons. He's the sort you find lurking in the poetry or philosophy section, depending on his chosen prey, muttering passages under his breath while stroking a perfectly manicured moustache. It's an approach that works depressingly well.

I prefer the slow burners. Shy eye contact across the table in the gender politics section one week, hands gently brushing in art and photography the next, standing slightly closer than expected in the queue at the counter, and finally a phone number slipped into a handbag.

You would be amazed by how many courtships begin with browsing. But if you think about it, where else outside of a bar can you get away with just hanging around? Glancing over and commenting on the book in your neighbour's hand is a perfectly acceptable way of starting up a conversation with a complete stranger. A bookstore can be a pick-up artist's paradise.

There is another group to watch out for. It's not always easy to tell them apart from the usual regulars but there are tell-tale signs if you know how to look for them. A slight awkwardness like they aren't comfortable in their own skin, pauses in the wrong places when they talk. They're the people who spend hours sitting in the customer chairs. They don't always buy the books they're reading, but spend enough money overall to not be considered time wasters.

They come to every single book launch, nursing a glass of wine and watching intently, but never mingling with the author or the other patrons. They are elderly and fragile, buried under trench coats and scarves. They are young and tattooed with garish coloured hair. The only thing they have in common in terms of outward appearance is that somehow, they don't quite fit into this world.

I remember the first time I met one. It was ten years ago, but still feels like yesterday. I was the only one left in the shop and about to close up when a woman rushed in, shaking and cradling a large handbag like it was her child. She asked if she could use the staff bathroom. Normally, the answer would have been no, but she was so clearly in distress that I grabbed the key and led her out the back.

As I guided her, I realised I recognised her as one of our regular sci-fi section browsers. I remembered her because of her clothing. In her mid to late forties, she would often turn up wearing some combination of fishnet stockings, Doc Martin boots, fairy skirt and rugby jersey. Most people wearing that sort of attire would be doing it ironically, but she always seemed free of affectation like someone who had chosen her clothes because she liked each individual item without giving much thought to the overall combination. That night she'd wrapped a large coat around her ensemble, which was why I didn't recognise her at first.

I was waiting in the hall outside the bathroom when I heard a crash and a wrenching cry. I raced in and forced the door open, for once actually pleased our boss had never got around to fixing the dodgy catch. She was lying on her side, wrapped around the foot of the toilet, groaning. As soon as she saw me, she grabbed her handbag again, trying to hide an obviously distended stomach. Naturally, my first thought was that she was about to give birth on our bathroom floor. I grabbed my phone to call 111, but she struck it from my hand, sending it skittering across the floor.

"No! Don't … unner…stan!" Her speech was laboured and slurred. Another groan escaped as she clutched at her belly, losing the grasp on the bag, which fell to the floor. The All Blacks jersey she was wearing had hitched right up and I could finally see what she'd been trying to hide. In place of the pregnancy bulge I was expecting was a face. Fused with her, or pushing out from the inside, was a forehead, eyes, nose and a mouth open in a silent scream.

What made it even more horrific was the fact it was a face I recognised. It was another one of our regulars. An elderly man who came by most Thursdays to sit in the reading corner with one of our international newspapers. He often took particular glee in judging us for not having read the books he was after.

The woman's eyes were black, and I mean completely black – no whites, no iris, just deep black voids. She had been wearing sunglasses when she came into the shop, which is why I hadn't noticed earlier. Giving up any pretence of hiding the monstrosity protruding from her belly, she collapsed onto her back, arms splayed out to the sides. "Should not happen … like this," she shook her head, struggling to find the words. "No pain, suffer he … not hurt …" As another bolt of pain rocked through her, she reached out. Out of impulse, I took her hand and squeezed it comfortingly, pushing a strand of greasy hair from her eyes. I had zero idea what was going on but I was certain she meant me no harm.

As her breathing began to slow, I let myself look down at her writhing body again. That's when I noticed the face was losing shape, shrinking as though it – he – was being absorbed. The longer I watched, the surer I became. His features were less defined, his bulging eyes sinking in. At the same time, her eyes were changing, lightening, the whites reappearing. The whole process couldn't have taken more than ten minutes, but the change was drastic. By the time the tip of our former customer's nose melted into the woman's now flat belly, she was sitting up, her eyes clear, sharp and full of fear.

She pulled down her jumper and looked at me, the power of speech returning. "You shouldn't have seen that. No one should ever see that! It shouldn't happen like that. I'm so sorry. I'm in so much trouble. I don't know what to do!"

I like to think of myself as a good judge of character and, despite what I'd just witnessed, what I saw right then was a scared woman who clearly needed my help. It also helped that I was a frequent flyer in our science fiction section as well, so, while I was repulsed and horrified, I was also a bit excited. One of my stories was coming to life and I wasn't going to let that kind of opportunity escape.

I could feel the strength return to her limbs as I helped her up off the floor, but the fear still hung in her eyes.

"You look like you could use a cup of tea," I said, steering her towards our break room. "I'll make you one and you can tell me what is going on and how I can help you."

Her kind don't learn like we do. They can't retain information for longer than five years. After that, everything they have absorbed disappears until they're left without basic human capabilities like speech or fine motor skills. 'Absorb' is the operative word. Every five years they choose a human to literally consume. During this process they take not just their knowledge on board but their basic humanity, giving them the ability to function in our world undetected.

And what better place to go cruising for human knowledge than in a bookstore? They try to pick people who won't be missed. They watch for those who have outlived their relatives or just live the type of quiet existence that their disappearance wouldn't be too disruptive. The somewhat unpleasant customer I watched my new acquaintance consume was one of those lonely sorts. His disappearance would probably have gone unnoticed until his bills started going unpaid. Some of their kind aren't quite so circumspect when it comes to choosing what they term 'donors' but mostly they don't want to draw attention to themselves. They spread their activities around book stores, libraries, galleries and museums in different towns and cities and try to stagger the weeks they take their donors. As far as I am aware, and I like to keep my ear to the ground when it comes to sci-fi conspiracy theories, they haven't been busted yet.

The process is supposed to be quick and painless for both parties, but, as I had witnessed, sometimes things don't always go smoothly. Me having witnessed the whole process was an absolute no-no and if my new acquaintance's indiscretion was discovered, … well, the outcome is best not imagined.

So, we struck a deal, she and I. I wouldn't call the police or let on that anything was amiss and she would point out which of my regulars were human-absorbing aliens in disguise (though I already had my suspicions). I would keep an eye on those folk and if I saw them getting too cosy with anyone I would be sad to see turned into goo, she would steer them away.

I agree, that sounds a bit callous, and definitely makes me complicit in murder but strangely it sits okay with me. I used to wonder if I related more to the creatures in the sci-fi books I love and now I'm almost certain it's true.

I mean nobody deserves to be dissolved into an alien life form, but when you are balancing on a chair, reaching for a book a customer has ordered, holding a phone in the other hand and being berated because you haven't read the latest Man Booker winner, sometimes, it's a little hard to be charitable. Just remember that, customers. A polite smile and a thank you might be all it takes to save you from a horrible fate.

The deal has worked well so far. In the past ten years, I've seen one 'donor' taken. This year will be my second. We've also had a new visitor. A stunning redhead who I recognised before she was even pointed out to me because of the way she didn't quite fit in her own skin.

I think it might be tonight. I caught a glimpse of her eyes through the sides of her glasses when she walked in, they're almost fully black. She has been taking quite an interest in the young man in the poetry section and I wonder if I should warn him.

Pretending to tidy up some shelves, I eavesdrop on their conversation.

"Do you come here often?" he asks her.

I think I'll let him figure that out on his own.

Nautical Nightmare

"I survived Wellington's nautical nightmare" is what's written on the t-shirts we sell to customers.

The nautical nightmare I have lived however would be beyond their wildest dreams.

Don't get me wrong, I wouldn't be in this business if I didn't like scary stuff. It's just usually it's me that's doing the scaring.

A couple of months ago, Wellington's Scare Factory officially opened. We're one of those haunted house type set-ups where people creep around in darkened hallways while we use live actors and special effects to scare the bejesus out of them.

It's my dream job really. I've always been a drama geek, but it wasn't until I took part in an interactive horror show, involving crawling under the audience's chairs and grabbing their ankles, that I discovered I really love scaring people. When the opportunity turned up to do it for a living, how could I possibly refuse?

I'm usually on front-of-house in my zombie make-up, but when we get victims – I mean customers – I'm needed out back on spook patrol. I won't go into too much detail – I don't want to give up all our secrets – but the screams and hysterical laughter we elicit from people make the whole enterprise worthwhile.

Before we got to the making-people-squeal stage though, we certainly had some start-up pains, which, now that I think about it, were probably the first signs that something was happening that wasn't quite the norm. It was mostly electrical stuff: lights flickering, air conditioning turning on and off, the Eftpos machines refusing service. Before we'd even opened, we began to feel like the place was jinxed.

I never admitted it, but they were unnerving thoughts while we were in the middle of making our décor as creepy as possible. We'd decided to go for a nautical theme, and my business partner Fred, who was obsessed with this sort of thing, went crazy on the research. He looked into historical stories about ghost ships, missing crews and creepy things that happened at sea, and we decided to theme the experience around a fictional ship that washed ashore minus its captain and crew after being missing for a year at sea.

Ours was a Frankenship based on the stories of several real ghost ships, and Fred, wanting to make things as authentic as he could, tried to make sure that as many of our creepy artefacts as possible were the real deal. He scoured second-hand chandleries and antique shops and car boot sales at yacht clubs for rusted anchor chains, old-school diving suits, rum barrels and fishing nets. His pride and joy was a terrifying looking doll in a sailor suit that an antique dealer – spotting a sucker a mile away – said was one of the only things that had washed ashore after the sinking of the Mikhail Lermontov.

A luxury Russian liner, the Lermontov hit the rocks in Port Gore in 1986 on the way out of the Marlborough Sounds, sinking like a stone after – to quote its captain – "a slight water intrusion." Despite the captain calling off the initial Mayday, thinking he could run the ship up onshore, repair and refloat it, a citizen's rescue involving fishing vessels, local yachts and an inter-island ferry, meant that all bar one of the Lermontov's 738 passengers and crew were rescued.

Being one of the world's largest shipwrecks, it is now a scuba site. Some of the most iconic images that came from the wreck are pictures of abandoned dolls on the floor of the ship's souvenir shop. Fred had some of those pictures printed and placed the doll (which I had named Chucky) between them. I had my doubts about the legitimacy of Chucky's origin story, but he certainly was creepy as hell.

We'd only been open for a couple of weeks when strange(r) than usual things started happening.

I was getting ready to close up. Most of my colleagues had left, but one had held back.

"That wasn't funny!" she whispered angrily once there were only the two of us left.

"What wasn't?" I asked, taken by surprise.

"Grabbing my ankle like that before. I got such a fright I almost broke character. That's how you get half-arsed performances!"

"Sharon, I honestly don't know what you are talking about," I said, trying to calm her down.

"Well, the others said it wasn't them, so it must have been you!" she said.

"I can honestly tell you, I didn't grab your ankle. I wouldn't do that. We're meant to scare the customers, not each other."

The poor thing looked utterly confused.

"I'll talk to the others tomorrow, okay?" I said.

Over the next week, other actors made similar complaints. Ankles grabbed, noises and moans in sections of the maze they were meant to be alone in, things whispered in ears that other people shouldn't have known.

Everyone was blaming each other, which wasn't making for a great working environment. I couldn't get a bead on who it was. Everyone seemed like they were telling the truth when they swore it wasn't them. Personally, I was convinced we had a very skilled trickster on board. We were all actors after all.

Then it happened to me.

Our last customers were going through for the night and I was lurking in one of my hiding spots, ready to get my spook on, when a sing-song voice whispered in my ear, "Georgie … Gee-oooorgie …" A high-pitched giggle followed.

I froze. Nobody had called me Georgie since I had been a scrawny kid being picked on for being different. My name was George. I was a grown man, an actor and a businessman – not a scared, bullied child.

"Georgie Porgie, pudding and pie … kissed the girls and made them cry … Nobody wants to kiss Georgieeeeeee …"

Another tinkling giggle.

I know creepy little girl laughter. Creepy little girl laughter is our stock-in-trade. For some reason, nothing can turn a grown adult to jelly like the sing-song voice of a pre-teen princess. We practice it during our lunch breaks. This, however, was unlike anything even the best of us had managed to produce.

There was something odd about her voice too, an accent that I couldn't quite place.

I shivered and not just with nerves. I was actually freezing cold. It was as if the temperature had suddenly plummeted several degrees. If it hadn't been so dark, I was certain I could have seen my breath.

A panicked scream, followed by a peal of hysterical laughter, made me both jump out of my skin and breathe a sigh of relief. The customers! What was wrong with me? Customer screams had never made me jump before. They are what I live for!

The temperature seemed to return to normal and I went about my usual routine, perhaps with a little less gusto than normal. I managed to control the shaking by the time we'd finished. I thought about having the rest of the staff up about it, but it was the Georgie thing that stopped me – and that rhyme! They couldn't possibly have known!

I waited until everybody had left, then turned on every single light in the building, before sorting out the till and getting ready to lock up. I felt ridiculous, but it helped calm my nerves.

I was just about to leave when the air turned chill again. I heard a soft, rhythmic noise. It took me a while to realise it was a child, quietly sobbing. I froze.

"Guys! This is seriously unfunny!" I said, trying to sound stern but struggling to keep the shaking out of my voice.

The sound was coming from our haunted maze. Feeling bolder with the lights switched on, I swung open the door and stormed back there.

"I'm sorry, Georgie … George!" the voice quickly corrected. "I didn't mean to be mean. I'm so lonely and I thought people liked being scared!" It said plaintively.

I charged around the maze, looking in every creepy nook and cranny, but found nothing.

"Please, George, make it dark again. I don't like the light!" the voice pined in my ear.

I spun around, there was no one there. A crash from the main room sent me running out of the maze. Lying on the floor by the counter were the two photos from the Mikhail Lermontov, along with Chucky, the creepy doll.

"His name's Charlie, not Chucky!" the disembodied voice corrected. "And he's not creepy, he's my best friend!"

Trying my best not to completely lose my mind, I picked up the doll to return it to its place on the counter.

As soon as I touched it, I collapsed to the ground, overwhelmed by visions.

Flash.

A woman in a dingy hospital bed, clearly dying, handing a doll in a sailor suit to a little girl. "This is Charlie," she said, in the same accent as the little girl – Russian, I realised. "Always keep him with you. He will look after you when I'm gone."

Pale, blonde and wearing a dirty white dress, the little girl clutched the doll to her chest, tears streaming down her face.

Flash.

A dusty room with multiple beds filled with malnourished looking children – an orphanage. Shouting and beatings and being forced to scrub and sew. The little girl pulling a suitcase from under her bed and packing her few belongings – some sandwiches swiped from the kitchen, another white dress and Charlie, the doll.

Flash.

The girl hiding near a wharf, watching the scurrying and excitement around a massive cruise ship. Watching as the staff, cooks, cleaners and engineers, bustled on and off, preparing the behemoth for its rich customers.

Flash.

Sneaking on board with the cleaners, who sometimes brought their children to work to see how the other half lived. Hiding in the laundry, sleeping on soft bedding and pillows for the first time in a long time. Scuttling from cupboard to hallway, remaining undetected until the ship set sail.

Flash.

Sneaking into the back of an on-board movie theatre, excitement at the movie – Gremlins – which she knows she's too young to be allowed to see. A crash and a graunch and the whole ship shudders to a halt. Alarms and then no alarms, life jackets and laughter. People suddenly leaving the theatre while the movie is still running. Staying behind to watch the rest – no adults to say she can't. Water coming in from nowhere, moving so fast she can't run or swim against it. Losing her grip on Charlie, the doll, who floats away out of reach.

I dropped the doll, gasping for air.

"The Mikhail Lermontov," I whispered.

"Yes," the voice said.

"But everyone survived!" I said. "Only one person didn't make it out, and he certainly wasn't a little girl."

"They didn't know I was there," she said. "Please, George, turn the lights off, so I can come out!"

Numbly, I stood up and did as I was asked, gently picking up the doll and the photos and placing them back on the counter.

It took a while before my eyes re-accustomed to the dark, and I was able to spot a pair of transparent feet and the hem of a dress poking out from the bottom of the door to the maze. I walked towards it slowly.

"You found me!" she giggled delightedly as she stepped forwards through the door.

She was tiny. I would've put her at about seven but with the build of a five-year-old. She had matted, damp looking hair – blond, I assumed. She was transparent after all – with twinkling eyes and a mischievous grin.

"What's your name?" I asked.

"Irina. Though most people call," she paused, correcting sadly, "people used to call me Rina."

"Well Rina it is then," I said.

Now that the shock had worn off, my professional saturation in all things spooky kicked in, making me more capable of rolling with the situation than most people.

"Why are you here, Rina?" I asked, knowing ghosts generally only hung about when they had unfinished business.

"To protect Charlie!" she said defiantly.

I smiled. I should have known Fred's artefact hunting obsession would land us with haunted shit at some point. "I promise we will take good care of Charlie," I said. "Is there somewhere you want me to take him?"

"No!" she said, suddenly animated. "You need to keep him close! We need to protect him!"

"From what?" I asked, thinking that at worst, we would have to move the doll to a lockable cabinet.

Before Irina could answer, a terrible crash echoed from behind the door to the maze, followed by a series of loud thumps that sounded like they were heading closer.

Thud. Thud. Thud.

"From him!" Irina finished.

Before I could ask any further questions, she disappeared through the door (which was still closed at this point, I might add) and an almighty ruckus ensued: Crashing, snarling, the whole building vibrating. I honestly can't tell you why I ran towards the noise instead of away from it, but that's exactly what I did. A few turns into the maze and I saw a towering figure with a long scraggly beard, twisted moustache and fiery eyes. Dressed like a 17th century pirate in a baggy shirt, long waistcoat and tricorn hat, a livid scar ran down one side of his face. When he opened his mouth to roar with rage, only a few jagged teeth were left.

He lunged at Irina, but she ducked out of the way just in time, leaving him running headlong through the walls. The building shook again as he lumbered back. I stared helplessly as the two faced off again, they were both transparent – what could I do?

The pirate ghost roared but before he could move, Irina let out an unholy shriek. I clamped my hands over my ears, but it was no use; her banshee wail pierced right through my soul.

I watched in fascinated horror as she, for want of a better word, expanded. Like Alice when she ate the side of the mushroom that made her grow tall. She was little girl and stretched monstrosity all at once. As she continued howling, her mouth elongated, stretching wider and wider until it was more than twice the size of the rest of her face. Stretching out of that gaping maw was row upon row of razor-sharp teeth. Paralysed with fear, I felt a warm trickle of urine run down my leg.

Clearly, the monstrous little girl was too much for the roaring captain, who stumbled backwards and disappeared.

I collapsed against the wall, tears I didn't even notice I had been crying drying on my cheeks.

"It's okay," Rina whispered, now back down to her normal size. "He's gone now. I've tired him out. He won't come back tonight."

I took a shuddering breath, trying to pull myself together.

"But he will come back," she finished sadly. "And I'm not going to be able to hold him off forever."

The next day at work, I was an absolute mess. The customers didn't notice, but it was obvious to the rest of the staff that something was up. Fred, the only person I would consider sharing this level of crazy with, was away on another artefact gathering mission, and it wasn't the sort of thing that could be explained over the phone. I was certain he would be spewing to be missing out on the action though.

I fobbed the others off by telling them I wasn't feeling well and offered to cover the front desk – the least-favoured job – for the whole shift while they handled the scares. Assuring everybody I would be fine, I offered to lock up again.

As soon as I was on my own again, the temperature dropped and a sweet voice whispered in my ear.

"I'm sorry he scared you," she said.

"You were pretty scary yourself, Rina," I said, spotting her bare feet poking through the bottom of the maze door again. "I know whose side I would rather be on!"

She giggled and I turned the lights near the counter down to encourage her to come out. Seconds later, she was perched cross-legged on the counter, next to her doll.

"So why does he want Chucky … sorry, Charlie so badly then?" I asked, eying the doll in its sailor suit.

"I don't know," she whispered. "But he does and he's getting stronger!"

As if on cue, the thumping started from the maze. This time it was faster like he was running. Thud. Thud. Thudthudthud.

Before I had the chance to think, the door swung open, crashing against the wall and knocking pictures to the floor. Lamps swung from the ceiling and rum barrels rocked from side to side. Irina screamed as Charlie levitated from the counter and slowly floated through the air towards the man who had suddenly appeared in the middle of the room.

"NO!" she screamed.

Out of reflex, I lunged for the doll and plucked it out of the air. An invisible force was trying to snatch it from my hands. It was like playing tug of war with nothing.

Irina floated about, snapping and snarling helplessly, clearly not prepared for the pirate's latest burst of strength. Clinging on to Charlie with all my might, I felt the fabric of his sailor suit rip and heard a loud clunk as something hit the floor.

Suddenly, the grip on the doll loosened. Still clutching him with all my strength, I scanned the floor for the source of the clatter, my eyes catching a glint of gold on the ground – a coin. I scooped it up and once again collapsed with the intensity of the visions washing through me.

Flash.

Poverty, hunger, rage. A man with the sense he deserved much more than a meagre sailor's wage.

Flash.

Guns and blood and stolen ships. Hapless crew members being tossed overboard.

Flash.

Listening while a fellow pirate drunkenly boasts about capturing a chest of gold from a Spanish treasure ship.

Flash.

Sneaking about his rival's ship in the darkness. Standing over him as he drunkenly snores in his bunk. Slitting his throat from ear to ear and taking the gold he rightfully deserves.

Flash.

Captain of his own ship now, ruling with an iron fist. Obsessed that someone will come for him to steal his gold. Sleeping with coins under his pillow. So focussed on protecting his riches, he fails to notice discontent brewing aboard. He wasn't prepared for the mutiny. Guns and blood and this time, he is the one being tossed overboard.

Flash.

Falling backwards into a violent sea. Watching his ship sail away from him. Clutching the last of the coins in his drowning hand. Losing his grip as he swallows a final lung full of water. Watching as the gold slowly sinks to the ocean floor.

Flash.

The 1980s. A woman, who has found out she is dying, walking by the seaside, spotting a golden glint in the sand. Picking up a coin and dusting it off, realising it's probably ancient. Talking with a friend, an antique dealer who values it for her on the sly.

"Keep this close, and tell no one. It's worth more than you can imagine. It will set up Irina for life."

Flash.

A mother sewing a gold coin into the hem of a doll's sailor suit, presenting it to her only child on her deathbed.

Finding myself on the floor once again, trying to catch my breath, my focus is drawn back to what's going on around me.

"Keep hold of the coin!" Irina is yelling, lunging and snapping at the pirate. "If he can't get near it, he'll weaken."

I watched helplessly as the pair wrestled, every ounce of energy sucked from me by the visions. It took all I had to keep my hand clamped around the coin.

Irina drew herself up to her full, terrifying form, snapping and snarling at the pirate until he backed right through the maze door and vanished.

"He's not coming back tonight," she whispered as she sat down on the floor next to me, an innocent little girl again.

I turned the coin over in my hand. "This was how Charlie was supposed to look after you," I said to her. "This is why your mother wanted you to keep him with you."

"Well, it's no use to me now that I'm dead," she said sadly. "And he looked after me in other ways. I found you!"

I rolled the coin between my fingers, thinking about pirates and their treasure. One of the things I learned from our background research was that the majority of pirates weren't actually sailing around with chests full of pieces of eight. Yes, they stole all the things, but it was mostly food, booze, clothing and parts for their ships. They mostly targeted ships transporting goods across the ocean. So, when they did find gold, it was precious indeed.

"I think he's tied to the coin, like you are to Charlie," I said to Irina. "And I think I know how we can send him away. Want to go on another boat ride?"

On my next day off, I boarded the Aratere Cook Strait ferry, a distant cousin of the Arahura – the ferry that came to the rescue when the Lermontov sank. Secure in my backpack was a sailor doll and a golden coin. Rina had told me that, while it was painful to make herself visible in the daylight, her presence would remain in the doll and she would be able to experience what was going on around her. It would be the same for the pirate, she said. He was there but during the day he was weak.

I waited until we were in the deepest part of the strait and headed out onto the ship's deck.

Feeling the heft of the coin in my hand, I can't say the thought of the fortune I was throwing away didn't run through my head for a second. But I pulled my arm back and hurled the treasure as far from me as possible.

The second it hit the water, I saw a weak, but unmistakably human shape dive in after it. The pirate fusing with the only thing that was ever important in his life.

A week later and work had returned to normal – or as normal as it can be when your office is a haunted house. No roaring, no thumping, no pictures flying off the walls.

After closing on Friday, I turned to Irina, who was in her usual cross-legged position on the counter.

"So, the Lermontov. You're still down there, right?"

"Yes, in the movie theatre."

"Do we need to send someone to find you, so you can rest for good?" I asked.

"Maybe one day," she said. "But not right now. I quite like it here and I like you."

I smiled. "I like you too."

She doesn't show herself every night, but most of the time I feel her presence.

Sometimes, when she's feeling mischievous, she'll help us with the customers. I've got her to hold back on the really scary stuff though, and no more spooking people with things she shouldn't know.

She can't help herself when it comes to messing with the staff either. She's still a kid after all. But she's gentler about it now. They are still blaming each other and I play along. It might be selfish, but I don't really want to share my little ghost friend.

One day, when she's ready, I will find a way to get someone down to the ship, so she can properly be put to rest, but I think that's still a while away. I can't see her getting bored with scaring Wellingtonians any time soon.

THE NIGHT I HELPED AN INTERSTELLAR BOGAN

It was 3am and all I wanted was a kebab – now, I'm the only person in Wellington who knows the reason behind the mysterious disappearance of the bucket fountain.

I'm an engineer. I work as a mechanic for a car shop out in Miramar that does a lot of bespoke stuff for rich plonkers with more money than sense, and we often end up working odd hours to get shit done. I don't mind though. The pay's good and I get to play with cool cars.

It often means that after work drinks are at stupid o'clock and end up going into the small hours of the morning – which is how I found myself stumbling down Courtney Place at 3am, desperately in search of a kebab.

You know when you get the drunk munchies and you fixate on one foodstuff to rule them all? Some weeks it's a pie, others fried chicken. That particular night it was a kebab. I was boozed enough to have convinced myself it was the healthy option. I mean they have salad in them after all! Though the version I was lusting over, the one with the hot chips wrapped up with the salad, meat and bread, probably not so much. One foot in front of the other, right-kebab, left-kebab, right-kebab … Barbecue sauce and Greek yoghurt and chilli, it was probably the only thing keeping me upright at that point in time.

Weaving across the footpath, I closed in on the kebab shop I knew would still be open at that time of the morning. I was only a block away from my heart's desire when I noticed a strange green glow coming from the gutter across the road.

Now, I've seen some weird shit wandering the streets of Wellington at sparrow's fart – vampires, werewolves, hobbits pissing in places they shouldn't – nothing was new to me. But this was actually different enough to divert me, if only briefly, from my kebab hunt.

I wobbled across the road, planning to check it out, add it to my 'weird shit in Wellington' ledger and get back on the road to sustenance. The green light was pulsing from something in a grey hoodie, sitting slumped in the gutter, head in its hands.

"S'up?" I asked, crashing down next to it.

Glow-dude looked up and its hood fell down. My blurred vision swam into focus – well, that was different!

It wasn't exactly the stereotypical little green man, but elements of that were there. It had an oval face and its eyes were definitely larger than the norm but not the pop culture dinner plates you see. Its nose was very small and narrow but it was still a nose like yours and mine. Its mouth was like ours too but smaller, like a child's mouth on an adult's face. The giveaway though was its skin, which was booger green and glowing in rhythmic pulses.

"Sssso, ya're an alien then?" I slurred.

"Yup."

"How you doon?"

"Drunk."

"Me too. Don ss-see many of your sort round here," I said, the alcohol numbing the shock I probably should have felt.

"See too many of your sort round here," Greenie replied.

"Donneed to be an A-hole about it. Juss being friendly," I said, attempting to lever myself up out of the gutter. "Stuff you mate, I'm gettin' a kebab."

The alien put an unsteady hand on my shoulder – three fingers and a thumb I noted – to stop me from leaving. "Sorry dude, I'm having a shit century. Didn't mean to take it out on you."

"Nuffin' a kebab can't fix," I said, feeling generous since it had made my night interesting. "Ssstay here. I'll get you one an' you can tell me what the problem is. I might be able to fix it, fixin' shit is what I do."

"Doubt it," the green grump replied. "But a kebab would be good."

"Ssay no more. I'll be right back," I slurred, making a less than graceful exit from the gutter. At least, I ended up on my feet.

I stumbled across the road, humming to myself as I entered the shop and placed my order – two large mixed kebabs with chips and all the good sauces.

Scoffing mine as I walked back across the road, I was glad to see my new acquaintance was still there.

"Here ya go, mate," I said, passing the holy grail of drunk comfort food.

"So, how long you been in Wellington?" I asked.

"Since 1969."

"Shit. How come no one's spotted you before?"

"People have, but they're usually wasted like you. So, no one pays them any mind. I tend to avoid going out until the small hours of the morning. There's a sweet spot between 4 and 4.30am when the last of the booze hounds go home or pass out and the street cleaners start up. I'm not usually on the street this early, but fuck it."

"So, what's your deal?"

"I'm stuck here. I crashed my ride."

"Aw shit," I said, feeling for it. The only thing that hurts more than having your wheels – or wings I assumed in this case – smashed is when you've done it to yourself.

The genuine sympathy in my voice must have thawed it a bit because it started getting into its story.

"Yeah, I'd just modded the ship up and was taking it out for a spin when a mate of mine challenged me to a race. I was absolutely creaming them when I hit the hyper-drive too hard, spun out of control and came crashing into this shithole. Been trying to fix it ever since."

"Dude, that sucks. How bad is it? S'pose there aren't too many spare parts for a space ship around here."

"Actually, you'd be surprised at how similar your vehicles are to ours, incredibly primitive of course, but close enough for a temporary patch up. I've got most of it back together, but no matter how hard I try, I just can't get the damned engine to turn. Might as well accept I'm going to spend my egg-laying years down here with you primates."

"Mind if I take a look at it?" I asked, professional curiosity piqued. "I'm pretty good with motors."

"Doubt you could handle this one, but why the fuck not? Things can't possibly get any worse."

It prised itself out of the gutter and when it got to its feet, I realised how little it was – probably only about four foot.

"Wot?" it said, catching me staring.

"Nothing mate – take me to your ship!" I said, grinning at how awesome that sentence sounded.

Less than five minutes later, we were standing in Cuba Mall, staring at the bucket fountain. For those of you not from the area; the Wellington bucket fountain is an iconic kinetic sculpture that is basically a bunch of giant primary-coloured Tupperware measuring cups. The 'buckets' fill with water until they get heavy enough to tip into the buckets below them, and so on and so forth until the water splashes down into a pool below. At least, that's the theory. In reality, Wellington's infamous wind grabs hold of the water before it has a chance to head downwards and throws it at passing pedestrians instead. The buckets can also empty with so much force that the water bounces back out of the pool and, again, over passers-by. Weirdly, everybody loves it.

"So, where's the ship?" I asked.

"Right here. At least the top of it is, the rest is underground."

"Wait, wait, wait …," I said, the kebab had soaked up most of the alcohol and I was beginning to sober up. Enough to realise how silly this was at least. "You're telling me the bucket fountain is actually a crashed alien spaceship?"

"Part of one," it finished. "That's just the top, it's much bigger down below."

"But I thought it was designed by some stoners in the 60s?"

"Yeah, there was a fair bit of mind washing needed to get your lot to believe that. Managed to convince people the crash was an earthquake too. You humans are so easy!"

"Okay, I'll bite. If this monstrosity is the top of an interstellar craft, what on earth is it for?"

My alien friend beamed. "State of the art wind scoops. They catch solar winds and increase the speed of your interstellar hyper-drive. The hyper gears only work in a straight line, but if you go round the outside of a planet and stick out the back some, you can slingshot off it and get your ship going sideways, which looks awesome!" it said. "You have to be careful though, because it can stuff up the navigation and if the planet you're circling gets in the way, you can end up crashing into it," it finished sheepishly.

"So, basically you crashed while space drifting?" I said, my inner boy-racer was very excited at this prospect.

"Pfft! You really think humans came up with drifting by themselves?"

"You're seriously not taking credit for that, are you?"

"Not me personally – let's just say I'm not the only one to have run into grief in this neck of space," it said. "Another of us did the same thing as I did, but crashed in a place called Japan. While looking for parts to fix their ship, they discovered the same principles of drifting in space applied to the more primitive human vehicles. They found a bunch of like-minded humans and made them a pet project. Now they go by the name Keiichi Tsuchiya and show no desire to go home. I, on the other hand, want the hell out of this dive."

My head was spinning – Keiichi Tsuchiya, the Drift King, was an interstellar bogan? Actually, it made a strange sort of sense.

"Okay then, so this is your space spoiler," I said. "Let's see the rest." I was trying to play it cool, but seriously, how often do you get to see the inside of a UFO? My mechanic spidey senses were tingling all over.

"Why do I feel like I'm going to regret this?" the alien asked. Then, "meh, why do I care?"

The cynical little bugger walked over to the giant Perspex tuatara that stands guard over the bucket fountain playground. In Wellington nothing says 'come and play' like a giant pre-historic lizard. Idly, I wondered if it resembled something from the creature's home planet.

It pressed one of the bumps on the tuatara's tail and quickly stepped back. The whole play area, slide and all, twisted anti-clockwise and lifted upwards to reveal what looked like a lift shaft below.

"Alright, come on then. Quickly! I don't like leaving the entrance up for the world to see."

I hauled my, still admittedly a little wobbly, arse over to the playground and joined the alien in the shaft. The whole process was eerily silent. No rattle and clank of pulleys and chains, just a door smoothly closing from the side and a silent glide downwards. When we hit the bottom, I heard a distant clunk from above us, the playground dropping back to its rightful place I assumed.

"Welcome aboard, human. Please don't lose the plot. Mind washing takes a lot of energy," the alien said.

I stood there, slack-jawed, staring upwards. We were at the bottom of a multi-story structure, floor after floor honey-combed above us, bathed in the same green light that pulsed from the creature. The structure was hexagonal but with no visible joins anywhere – a huge metallic creation, seemingly with no beginning and no end. Below us, I could hear a soft rumbling.

"It's beautiful," I whispered.

The creature pulsed a little brighter, with pride I suspected.

"Well, given the primitive state of what you creatures are tooling around in, I'm not surprised this baby is a bit over-whelming," it said. "The engine room is down here by the thrusters, though I don't expect you'll be able to make head or tail of our mechanics."

To access the engine room, I had to almost bend myself in half. Designed for a four-foot creature, my six-foot bulk made things pretty cosy. Once I got in though, I would have put up with any amount of discomfort to stay. The engine was made of the same seamless material as the rest of the ship, its components linked together almost organi-cally. It glistened and pulsed, like a human body on an operating table. At the same time, I could see it had the same basic structure as our engines – crankshaft, pistons, connecting rods – just melded together as one whole. I could also see where it had salvaged parts from earth cars –

a fuel injector here, a valve there, melded in with the alien mechanisms.

The soft humming I heard when we boarded was a generator-type contraption. Pulsing and glowing green, it kept the ship powered while the engine was down, the alien said.

I asked what it ran on, but it said if it told me, it would have to vaporise me. Given that less than an hour ago, I'd found the creature drunk in a gutter, I wasn't entirely sure whether it was serious, so decided to change the subject.

"So, what appears to be the issue?" I asked.

"I start it up. It makes a noise. Then it stops," the alien replied grumpily.

"Well, crank her up then. Let's see if I can spot the problem."

"Righto," the alien said, lack of faith in my abilities oozing out of every little green pore. "You're gonna need these."

It handed me what were basically alien ear muffs, made of the same seamless material as everything else on the ship. I turned them over in my hands, marvelling at their craftsmanship.

"Just put them on," it muttered, rolling its golf ball eyes.

I managed to get them on just in time. A low rumble became a giant roar and the whole world shook for a few seconds.

"That one will register on Geonet," the creature said proudly. "That's all I can get out of her though," it finished dejectedly.

"So, it revs for a bit but won't start?" I asked, once my ears stopped ringing, "And it's not the battery?"

"I assure you, energy is not the issue," it said smugly. "We don't stoop to anything as vulgar as batteries."

"Fine, no need to be a prat about it. Sounds like the starter motor to me," I said.

The creature looked at me blankly.

"These things have starter motors, don't they?" I asked.

"Of course!" it said defensively. "I had to replace it with one of yours though, deeply inferior! We don't have starter motor issues in space."

"Well, you're not in space, you're on Earth and you've been here for a bloody long time."

"In your terms maybe," the creature muttered.

"In starter motor terms too," I finished. "Let's have a look at it."

The creature peeled back part of the amorphous silver engine bay and there it was, a garden variety human starter motor, attached on either side by silver tentacles, almost as if on life support.

"Well, I think that's your problem right there," I said. "Got any tools?"

"Do you really think that you can fix it?" the alien asked, its derision replaced with a mix of despair and a little hope.

"If it is what I think it is, then quite possibly yes," I said. "I'm going to need some tools and you're going to need to disconnect it from that silver stuff, that bit's definitely beyond me."

Happily feeling superior again, the creature leaned over the engine and gently pinched the metallic substance on either side of the starter motor. The connections shrunk back, as if letting go of their own accord. The alien plucked the motor out of the engine and passed it to me.

It felt incredibly strange holding something as banal as a starter motor while standing inside an alien spaceship. I crouched down on the floor, relieved at not having to duck in the tiny space any more, and began to examine the motor.

"Got a hammer?" I asked.

The creature just looked at me.

"You know, a hitty thing – or are you space folk too fancy for those?"

"You're telling me your big solution is to hit it with a hammer!?" it asked derisively.

"It's worked before. When the starter motor used to crap out on my Granddad's Ferguson tractor it was usually because the brushes had jammed. We'd just give it a couple of good whacks with a rock and it would be as good as new. If you don't have a hammer, I can go back up and find a rock," I said.

"I've got a hammer!" the alien said, stomping off and returning moments later with a large silver egg.

It tapped the oval with a single green finger and an opening appeared out of nowhere. I still couldn't see any joins. It was as if it was some sort of solidified silver liquid. The opening revealed a set of tools made of the same liquid silver, some that vaguely resembled ours and others so odd-looking I couldn't begin to fathom what they did. I rifled through the tool egg, pushing aside its sonic screwdriver collection in exasperation. Which one of these bloody things was a hammer?

The alien smirked as it watched, clearly enjoying how at sea I was with its fandangled tools.

Finally, I found it at the bottom of the egg, shiny and silver like everything else but otherwise your bog-standard thumb detector.

Waving the tool triumphantly, I turned to the starter motor.

The alien rolled its googly eyes in disbelief. "I've been trying for decades to get this thing going. I've tried every-thing, and you really think …"

"Have you hit it with a hammer?" I interrupted.

"No."

"Then you haven't tried everything. Now pipe down and let me work my magic."

Before ET could object, I grabbed the hammer, gave the motor three good whacks, added a fourth for good measure and gave it a shake. The brushes certainly seemed to have loosened up.

I handed it back to the alien, who was staring at me in horror. "Hook her up again and give it a try," I said.

Shaking its head in disbelief, the creature placed the starter motor back in the engine bay, stroking the silver material, which slithered back around to hold it in place.

It tossed the earmuffs to me and, this time, I put them on straight away.

The engine shuddered and sputtered and shook, and then it began to purr. That is the closest I can come to describing the sound – the rich, chocolaty purr of a giant contented cat that was shaking the world in its mouth.

The alien's own mouth had stretched as far as it could in an almost grin. "Let's get out of here, my beauty," it whispered – clearly not to me. The lights on the floors above us began to pulsate and glow with more force.

"You'd better get out of here," the alien said. "If you try to hitch a ride, the air pressure in here will squash you like a ripe tomato and, believe it or not, that would make me sad."

Quickly shunting me towards the shaft and pressing a button on the side, it sent me upwards. As the silver door closed, it looked me in the eye. "You did good – for a human," it said.

I was propelled upwards, the door sliding open and spilling me out onto the playground. The world trembled as the bucket fountain rose.

Bracing myself on the tuatara, I watched as what seemed like miles of gleaming silver erupted from the ground, primary coloured buckets spinning at its tip. It all seemed to happen in slow motion, but in fact, it was only seconds later that I was standing next to a gaping, fountain-shaped hole, watching a bright green light blink and flash as it headed towards the stars.

My ears rang as the roar of the take-off switched to an unholy screech, followed by what I could only assume was a sonic boom. The light flashed brighter, before rapidly changing direction twice and disappearing in a massive cloud of space smoke. Wellington's bucket fountain departed the city in a glorious space burnout.

When the ground stopped shaking, I stumbled to my feet and got the heck out of there. The last thing I wanted was to be the first person on the scene after that. Minutes later, I was sitting down at a bus stop on Courtney Place, smiling up at the stars. I couldn't say for certain but I liked to think, that last little bit of theatrics was his way of saying goodbye.

THE WONDROUS ADVENTURES OF MITTENS

Oh Mittens! You glorious ginger floof! I've spent so long trying to track you down and now that I've finally found you, I don't know what to think about anything anymore.

If you live in Wellington Central, chances are you've heard of, if not met, Mittens. Mittens, the Cat of Wellington, is a fluffy, friendly ginger cat who pretty much runs the place. He has a perfectly good home and loving humans but, like all cats, he goes where he wants – and where he wants is the whole damned city.

Mittens walks into people's offices and curls up on their printers. He goes into clothing stores, finds the blackest item he can and has a good long nap on it, leaving a Mittens-shaped pile of orange fur in his wake. He has visited the local police station, walked into people's houses and slept on their beds and is often seen curled up on the comfiest looking donation in the Willis Street Salvation Army window. He was once removed from, and snuck back into, the Michael Fowler Centre at closing time the night before the opening of Cats – he made the local papers for that one.

Mittens' evening antics are just as interesting – he's been spotted lurking in the trees outside a local strip club. And when he took a nap on a sofa onstage at a local music venue and refused to move for the band, he was carried offstage, sofa and all, with a 'Reserved for Mittens' sign placed next to him.

People marvel at his road sense with many commenting on how he appears to wait for the traffic signals before crossing the road.

In the early days before his fame spread, he was dropped off at the local SPCA so many times, a hotline was set up connected to a number on his collar: "This is Mittens. He has a home. He's not lost. Please don't feed him." This is all his humans ask his many fans – feel free to love and fuss over our incredibly social cat but don't feed him. Food time is when he knows to come home to us.

Mittens is perhaps most well-known through his Facebook page 'The Wondrous Adventures of Mittens.' There, people post photos and videos of their Mittens sightings and encounters, even selfies. They call him their 'King' and describe meeting him as being 'blessed'. "I was blessed today." "Our office was blessed." On occasion, Mittens' humans kindly post pictures of him home safe and sound, which make his followers very happy.

There are thousands of these images, probably tens of thousands by now. At the time of writing, Mittens' Facebook page had 45,000 members. Which was why I, a confirmed crazy cat lady, had my nose seriously out of joint that I hadn't been blessed. I moved in the same circles as Mittens, frequented the same shops and bars, but not so much as a glimpse of fuzzy ginger butt. I felt like I was the only person in Wellington that hadn't met the King and I was right royally pissed off.

So, when I finally caught a glimpse of a fluffy tail snaking down a side street near Cuba mall last week, my heart sang. Not wanting to spook him, I quietly tip-toed up to where I'd spotted him enter the alleyway and peered around the corner. Sure enough, there was His Majesty, strutting down the street – a cat on a mission. Cell phone camera at the ready, I hung back a bit, just out of sight, and followed him. Wherever he was headed, he was taking a circuitous route, nipping from one street to the next, doubling back on himself. At one point, I only just managed to duck into a shop doorway as he looked back over his shoulder as if he was aware, he was being followed.

Finally, I found myself round the back of the Light House Cinema, which was closed for the evening and, I assumed, locked up. I was wrong. Mittens confidently walked up to a side door, jumped up on his hind legs and pushed with his front paws. The door, which had clearly been left unlocked, swung inwards and Mittens let himself in.

Now, I know it was technically trespassing, but there was no way I was going to let this one go. I had a genuine mystery here and I was going to get to the bottom of it. Quickly checking over my shoulder to make sure no one was watching, I opened the door as silently as I could and commenced operation "Follow That Cat".

I'd managed to get in just in time to spot a fluffy tail disappearing around a corner. I quickly crept up behind him and followed as quietly as I could. It didn't seem to matter though as he was so intent on getting to his destination, I doubt he would have noticed me at all.

A couple of twists and turns later and we were entering the back of one of the theatres. I lost sight of him for a minute but what I saw once my eyes adjusted to the darkness made me forget about Mittens entirely.

The front six rows of the theatre were entirely filled – with cats. Cats sitting on the back of seats, cats curled up on the floor, cats wearing collars, cats that were obviously strays. And there, sitting in the front of the screen, was Mittens. I ducked behind a seat, peering out into the aisle so I could see what was going on. A massive tabby walked up to the front of the theatre, dragging what appeared to be a tablet in its mouth. It dropped it at Mittens' feet and jumped back down to join the feline throng. Mittens batted at the screen with his paw and it lit up.

Suddenly, the movie screen flickered to life. I looked around behind me to see if there was anyone in the projector booth but could not sense any human presence. The screen was a mess of colours and lights, swimming fish and darting critters – one of those games you can download to your device for your cats to play with. It flickered and then split into dozens of smaller screens, all showing similar things, cat games and nature shots of birds and squirrels – the type of Cat TV I leave on when I know my fur-child is going to be home alone for a while.

I smiled, thinking that while what I was witnessing was a little unnerving, it was quite adorable. Then the screen flickered again. Each game or TV show was replaced by a cat, a hundred plus pairs of eyes peering intently into the theatre.

I focused on the cats on the screen looking in. There, at the top left. Could it be? It was hard to say for sure but it certainly looked like my cat. I wracked my brain – had I left Cat TV on this morning? Yes, I had.

Mittens swatted at the tablet screen with his paw again, and this time, the whole movie screen filled with Facebook, specifically 'The Wondrous Adventures of Mittens' page. Another swipe and we were looking at the group's photo page, the latest Mittens sightings, selfies with the King. A third swipe and we were looking at a folder filled with hundreds of those pictures and then, more frighteningly, what was behind them – our data. The times the pictures were taken, GPS coordinates, the type of devices they were taken on.

The next screen showed a map with pinpoints all over the city and, hovering above those pins, images of Mittens, or people with Mittens. My heart was pounding in my throat and ears. They were marking our movements, collecting our data – data we were giving so freely every time we sought out His Royal Highness. They knew where we went and when. What on earth did they need it for? They were cats? What could they possibly be planning?

Another swipe at the tablet, and the face of a jet-black moggy appeared on the big screen, moving closer and closer until the entire theatre could see up a pair of gigantic nostrils. It took me a few seconds to register that the cat was tapping the screen with its nose.

The somewhat disturbing view of feline nasal passages was replaced with targeted advertising data for Nigel's Nip, a company that promised "potent strains for feline connoisseurs". A synchronised purr arose from the theatre cats.

The black nose reappeared and Mittens swiped at the tablet again. This time Calico filled the screen and the ad data was for dried sardine cat treats.

I watched as feline faces cycled on the screen, accompanied by social media advertising statistics. The ads ranged from the relatively benign – cat toys, scratching posts and Fancy Feast – to the more sinister – dog muzzles and shock collars – and the outright creepy – DIY underground bunkers and sporting equipment that could easily double as weapons.

Clearly, they were harvesting our data for targeted advertising, which was unnerving in itself, but the things the advertising was for? I could handle the nip and the treats, and the dog deterrents made sense, but what about the rest of it? What could they possibly need it for? They were cats!

The terrifying organisation of it all was broken, however, by the fact that pretty much one in every three cats was licking their butt or in a dead sleep by the time it was their turn on screen.

The theatre cats stared at the screen for a while and then each other. Aside from the odd chirrup and purr, the room was eerily silent. Interestingly, it has recently been discovered that cats don't meow at each other. They will hiss and spit and yowl when they fight and chirp and purr when they hang out together, but the meows are reserved for people. There are a bunch of theories about this, including that they are trying to get a reaction by mimicking a human baby's cry. Having witnessed what I just did, that wouldn't surprise me at all.

Mittens swiped the screen again and it switched back to the grid view of the watching felines who stared back knowingly. As the screen went blank, I realised it would be my only chance to get out unnoticed. So I quietly backed out of the theatre, crept down the hallway and let myself out. I quickly made my way to Cuba Mall and wandered the street, looking into shop windows like any other human noodling around town.

When I didn't see a mass exodus of cats (of course they would be smart enough to leave in dribs and drabs to avoid detection), I jumped on a bus and headed home, my head spinning. So many questions. What did they need with bunkers and baseball bats? Are there humans in on this? Surely, there must be for the door to be left open? Do I want in on this? What was I supposed to do?

I unlocked my door and was met by my cat, chirping a welcoming greeting and winding her way around my legs. I picked her up and she snuggled into my arms, looking up at me with eyes that always made me feel comforted and happy, even if she was biting me because I had pissed her off. Eyes that I couldn't possibly fear. I kissed her soft forehead, gave her chin a scratch and plopped her back down on the floor.

I've decided. Whatever is going on here, I for one welcome our feline overlords.

You Can't Beat Wellington on a Good Day

"Give those back you bastard, bastard, bastard wind!"

The man's suit jacket flapped behind him like a superhero cape as he chased his papers down the street. I giggled slightly to myself as I ran to help him gather them up. He grinned sheepishly when I passed over a handful of documents. "Wellington!" he sighed in exasperation and we shared a knowing look.

Most Wellingtonians have a love/hate relationship with our signature element. The scourge of washing lines, terror of trampolines and reason we can't have nice outdoor furniture, or umbrellas – the twisted skeletons of which were often seen inside out and poking up from rubbish bins. I've seen an open umbrella haring down the street by itself, no owner chasing after it. A friend of mine once spotted a pair of pants walking down the waterfront with no human inside.

When all that's said and done though, we are fiercely proud of our city – wind and all. "You can't beat Wellington on a good day," we say to anyone who will listen. If you can tolerate the occasional gale force tantrum, the city will reward you with a single, perfect, jewel-like day which makes it all worthwhile. It's part of living in and loving this city. Or at least it used to be. Somewhere along the line, things changed.

The first murder of that summer was at a bus stop. An argument over a delayed arrival got out of hand. The perpetrator was a policy analyst, who pled guilty immediately. He had a completely clean record. His family, friends and colleagues were shocked and he himself had no real explanation for his behaviour. One minute, he was in the midst of a heated discussion and the next, the red mist descended and he had his hands around another man's throat.

This was the beginning of a flood of unlikely killers – policy wonks and politicians, teachers and florists. A particularly nasty brawl that broke out in a rest home between the residents and the girl guides who were there to sing for them had to be broken up by the police riot squad. News reports about Wellington grew increasingly grim. Domestic violence rates were up, road rage incidents were on the rise. It was as if the entire city woke up one morning in an unfathomable, unnatural rage.

Nobody mentioned the good days anymore.

I was more careful when I went into town and stopped making eye contact with strangers, but for a long time, it was only on the periphery for me. I felt a sort of sadness for the state of our once vibrant city, but it wasn't until I was paying one of my regular visits to my great aunt Polly that things really hit home.

Polly's cottage was just a block away from our old family home in Island Bay. As a kid, I was obsessed with my great aunt. As far as I was concerned, she was the fount of all knowledge. I was one of those precocious kids who needed to know everything about everything immediately. I'm certain Polly's presence was a huge relief for my Mum, who would often send me down for visits. I suspect to get a break from the incessant "what's that? What for? Why?"

"Why don't you ask Aunt Polly?" was a common phrase in our household. She was technically my great aunt, but that was a bit of a mouthful for a toddler, and "Aunt Polly" stuck.

Luckily for Mum, Polly was more than happy to answer my questions and fill my head with knowledge of her own.

"Did you know?" followed by whatever I had learned from Polly that day replaced the whys and what fors. I don't know which was more annoying actually. I must ask Mum one day.

Polly taught me all about Wellington. About its storms and its shipwrecks and where the shoreline used to be. She showed me which local plants were poisonous and which could fix a tummy ache when brewed into a tea. We would go for walks along the beach and she would tell me which shells belonged to which critters. Most importantly though, she taught me about the wind.

It was on one of our beach walks that Polly first told me about listening to the wind. I had found a shell on the sea shore and excitedly pressed it to my ear to see if I could hear the ocean like I'd heard about from some kids at school.

"That's not actually the ocean you hear, dear," Polly said to me softly. "It's the sound of the air around you made bigger because it is echoing inside the shell."

Seeing my look of disappointment, she knelt down to my level and whispered conspiratorially, "Don't be upset. I can show you something much better."

Instead of listening for an ocean that wasn't really there, Aunt Polly taught me to listen for something that most definitely was.

I know it sounds rather obvious. I mean everyone can hear the wind, especially around here. It whistles and it howls and it knocks things about. It's not exactly subtle. But there's a layer underneath that, and that's what Polly showed me.

If you try hard, and at first it is really hard, you can hear more than just air rushing past. It sounds silly but it's almost like words. People talk about the wind whistling and howling, and that's exactly right. It does all of those things. But on a good day, you can hear it sing.

Aunt Polly and I would go for walks up into Wellington's hills on windy days. Mum would fuss and wrap me up in jackets and mutter about why we couldn't do it on a nicer day. Polly showed me the wind's emotions. When it whistled, it was happy. Those were the kind of windy days where there was a sort of a spark in the air, when you were full of energy and excitement but you weren't entirely sure why. When it howled, it was angry. Those times could be scary but also strangely cleansing, like it was blowing all the anger and rage of the earth somewhere far away.

It was on one of those howling days that Polly taught me that I could talk back. I'd had a rough day at school. I would sometimes get picked on for being a little different from the other kids. Most of the time, I could handle it, but that day had been particularly wretched. Mum was working late that afternoon, so I went straight to Polly.

She took one look at my tear-stained face and grabbed her jacket. "We're going for a walk," she said.

It was an absolute belter that day. Polly and I were forced to cling to each other as we clambered through bush and over rocks. Once we reached the peak of one of the hills, we looked over the bay down to Polly's cottage.

"Okay, tell me about it," she said.

I blurted the whole miserable episode out. "Normally, I can ignore them," I sputtered, the wind ripping the words from my mouth. "But it just got to me today. They were being such bitches!" I glanced over at Polly, expecting a reprimand. I'd never said the B-word in front of her before. But she said nothing. In fact, I could have sworn I'd seen a little smile.

"I know I should be better than them but I just can't be that all the time!" I sobbed.

"You don't have to be perfect all the time," Polly said. "It's not healthy. It was a crappy situation and you're allowed to feel angry about it."

My eyebrows just about rose right off my head.

"Especially when they are being such …" she paused, a wicked grin spreading across her face as she waited for me to finish.

"Bitches," I said, quietly but firmly.

"Say it again," she said. "Louder this time."

"Bitches!" I said, raising my voice.

"That's it!" she said, joining me. "BITCHES! BITCHES! BITCHES!" she yelled savagely into the wind.

The wind swirled around us, ripping away our words as we danced and swore and howled like a couple of crazed banshees. I could have sworn the wind's own howls were forming words.

"Be angry. It's allowed. I am too. Be angry. It's allowed. I'll take it away."

Utterly spent, Polly and I collapsed on the hillside, the wind still crashing around us.

"Thank you," I whispered. To Polly and the wind.

It was on that day that I became BFFs with the scourge of brollies city-wide. I loved nothing more than to go for a walk on a day when the wind was singing, listen to it tell its stories and sometimes, when I was on my own, sing back.

When I had bad days that coincided with stormy days, I would climb up to the highest point I could access and scream my troubles into the void. It was a dance of joy and rage and power.

***

At 102, Polly is still going strong – a little frail but a lot tough. I visit her as often as possible and it was on one of those visits that Wellington's new insanity came crashing into my life.

Before I even managed to get a third knock in, the door was wrenched inwards and there was Polly, brandishing a carving knife, her eyes burning and her slight frame trembling with rage. Instinctively, I jumped back, just in time, as she lunged towards me with a surprising amount of speed and power.

"Aunt Polly!" I said, trying to calm her – and myself. "It's me!"

It was no use. Her glazed eyes barely registered me as she swung around, stabbing in my direction.

"You won't take me! I'm not going! I'm coming out of here feet first, you motherfuckers!" she screamed.

My legs were trembling and tears sprung to my eyes, an involuntary sob wrenched from my lips. Whoever this was, it was not my aunt.

"No one is taking you anywhere, Polly," I said, hands up in surrender as I tried to lead her back towards the house. "Let's sit down and talk this over."

It must have been my tears that snapped her out of it. She dropped the knife and collapsed to the ground.

"Oh, oh! I'm so sorry!" she said, tears pouring down her cheeks. "I don't know …"

"It's okay, Polly," I said, gently helping her up. "Let's just get you inside."

Both in shock, I steered her towards her favourite arm-chair and busied myself in the kitchen, where I could still keep an eye on her, making us both a cup of tea.

I was scared and confused. As far as I was aware, there had only ever been one conversation between my mother and Polly about her going into care, and it ended the way we all thought it would. Mum really only suggested it because she felt obliged to point out there could be an easier way of life, but we all knew the old woman would never willingly leave that cottage. I had no idea what had put it in her head now.

I passed Polly her mug and sat in the chair opposite. Her eyes had cleared, and all I saw was confusion and contrition.

"I don't know where that came from. I really don't," she said. "Everything's just got so … heavy. Sometimes I feel like everyone is out to get me. I get so scared I can't breathe. Would you mind opening the window, dear? Let a little air in?"

I squeezed her hand and got up to open the window but I knew it would be in vain. There would be no fresh air. Wellington had been uncharacteristically still for a long time.

"How long have you been feeling like this, Aunt Polly?" I asked. "Be honest."

"Probably about three months," she said sheepishly. "I didn't want to worry you or your mother."

"Three months is a long time to feel out of sorts," I chided gently, not wanting to upset her more than she already was. I settled myself back into my chair, now sticky with humidity. To be honest, I was a bit on edge, too. I hadn't slept for a long time. The nights had been so muggy. It felt like Wellington had been like this forever, heavy and still and sullen. How long had it been? I wondered, an idea formulating in the back of my mind.

I pulled out my phone and checked the latest 'Why is there no wind?' story in the media. 'Record drought continues … no wind and rain for three months.'

For three months, our city had been hot, muggy and listless. Crops were drying out, yachts stayed put in the marina and nobody slept.

I did another search, heart pounding. Three months ago, almost to the day, Wellington's first unexplained murder. The man at the bus stop. We'd had three months of darkness, violence and rage.

It sounded crazy but, in a way, it made perfect sense. For three months, we had been without our identity. We complain, but the wind is Wellington's fierce beating heart. Without it, we don't know who we are. It's our lungs. It blows away our anger, pain and sadness and for three months, it had been holding its breath.

I cast my mind back to before I stopped hearing the wind sing. We'd had a few decent blows in quick succession. Power lines downed, seawalls breached, one man tragically killed when his car was crushed by a falling tree branch.

Mostly, it was frustration though. Our language around the wind had changed. People were busy and didn't have time for its shenanigans. Knowing smiles had been replaced by curses. We hated it. We wanted it to stop. When I thought about it, the vitriol against the wind had been the worst I'd ever heard.

I showed Polly what I had found. Her eyes widened.

"I think it's on strike," I whispered incredulously.

She just looked at me.

I was certain now, and what's more, I was angry. "The wind has been sulking for the last three months and it's destroying our city. The selfish shit!"

Polly, the old Polly – my Polly, was grinning at me, eyes sparkling.

I stood up and grabbed my jacket, heading for the door.

"I think it's time someone told it to pull its head in," I snapped.

Polly pulled herself up to come with me. I took one look at her 102-year-old frame and shook my head. "Not this time, Polly. You've taught me everything I need to know. I'll sort this one out myself. Don't get into any trouble before I get back," I finished sternly, closing the door behind me before she could talk her way into the expedition.

Sweating, panting and cursing the fact I hadn't had the forethought to bring a water bottle, I clawed my way to the highest point of the hills behind Polly's cottage.

I stood for a moment, catching my breath and surveying the bay and the city, all the tiny people in their tiny houses. I thought of the anger and the pain and the death. I thought of Polly in her cottage, alone and angry and not knowing why, and I screamed at the top of my lungs.

It was a ragged, raw, painful scream that echoed across the hills. I was angry too, but I knew exactly what I was angry at.

"WHAT. THE. FUCK?" I screamed, not caring if anyone could hear. "WHAT DO YOU THINK YOU'RE DOING?"

I screamed again, a burning, guttural cry of rage. I spat and snarled; a woman possessed.

"WHY?"

Nothing.

I collapsed to the ground sobbing, laying on my back with my eyes squinted closed against the sun. Exhausted, my breathing finally slowed, and as it did, I felt something prickling at the back of my mind.

It was pain. Pain and then anger. It was a barrage of constant curses and snide remarks. It was hearing it was hated thousands upon thousands of times. I lay there, not even trying to wipe away the tears streaming down my face.

Sitting up, I looked around. Not a whisper. Everything was achingly still.

"It's not true," I rasped, my throat raw from screaming. "We need you. Yes, people can be arseholes, but they're just people. You're the wind!"

Still nothing.

"Have you seen what this city has become without you? People are dying!"

A flash of an old man, dead in his crushed car.

"That's different!" I yelled, my energy creeping back. "That sort of thing happens. That's nature. You're nature! What is happening now is the opposite of natural!"

I thought of Polly and the men at the bus stop. The man who was murdered and the one who might as well have been.

"Alright!" I yelled. "You've made your point! Do you want us to beg? Watch the news, we fucking are! Are you really going to let a bunch of bipedal bullies win? You're the fucking wind!"

I could have sworn I felt a tiny gust. It only stirred my rage.

"Blow, you coward!" I screamed.

The prickle in the back of my head turned into an angry surge. 'Good!' I thought. 'Let it get mad. I'm mad.' The pain became intense. I ignored it.

"Are you mad?" I screamed, heaving myself up from the ground and flinging my arms wide. "Come on then. Knock me down. Come on, you coward. Fight me!"

A stabbing pain behind my eyes. I doubled over but stood firm. I thought back to the first time Polly took me up into the hills in a gale. How upset I was, how the wind blew away my pain and rage. I thought of the words I heard in the wind's howls and I shouted them into the air, spinning around and around.

"Be angry. It's allowed. I am too. Be angry. It's allowed. I'll take it away."

I felt a strength grow in me as I recited the words like a mantra. "Be angry. It's allowed …"

I thought of the silly schoolgirl fight and of all the bullies in the world, of the people cursing and hating.

"BITCHES, BITCHES, BITCHES!" I screamed, electricity crackling around me as I turned faster and faster.

I didn't notice at first that the rage building up inside me had burst outwards. It wasn't until I slowed my spinning to catch my breath that I saw the sky had begun to darken, that the branches around me were beginning to sway. It had been so long, I had almost forgotten what the sound was.

I felt the wind's rage building up around me.

"Come on then!" I taunted. "If you're so pissed off, knock me down! Do it!"

It did.

One minute, I was shouting at the sky and the next, I was on my arse gasping for breath and grinning like an idiot.

"Yes!" I howled wildly. "Harder! Stir us up! Blow all the shit away!"

The wind finally obliged. I heard an almighty crack as the limb from a tree behind me crashed to the ground. Leaves spun through the air as I braced myself against a rock on the hillside.

I let go, stumbling blindly down the hill, spinning in erratic circles.

"Be angry. It's allowed. I am too."

Grasping at tree trunks as I made my way back down to Polly's cottage, I pushed myself against the gale. I looked up at the clouds racing across the sky and smiled.

You can't beat Wellington on a good day, and today was a good day.

ABOUT THE AUTHOR

Anna Kirtlan is a short, brightly coloured cat enthusiast. Her fiction is a mix of sci-fi, fantasy, horror and humour, often with a nautical bent. Her non-fiction work focusses on mental health advocacy and attempting to sail.

You can find more about Anna's work and read her blog as seamunchkin.com, follow her on Instagram and Twitter as @Seamunchkin and join her Facebook page 'Anna Kirtlan writes'.

Also by this author
WHICH WAY IS STARBOARD AGAIN?

Published 2015 by David Bateman Ltd
batemanpublishing.co.nz
ISBN 978-1-86953-881-1

Captivating yachting tale that's not all plain sailing.

When sailing novice Anna Kirtlan takes to the high seas, expect the unexpected. Not many people have the courage to sail the South Pacific with as little experience as Anna, who not only has to learn to sail from scratch, but also to overcome the anxiety attacks that have plagued her since her teens. She is upfront about living with mental illness and of being scared out of her mind but somehow doing it anyway. With humour and insight Anna relates the adventures she shares with her partner Paddy on board Wildflower and the characters they meet along the way.